NOT  THE SEASON

EMILY NICOLE

Edited by Gabby D'Aloia at GCD Editorial
Character art by Ivanna Nashkolna
Cover design by Emily Nicole
Formatting by Talia Aden

Website: emilynicoleauthor.com
Instagram: @emilysbookedup

For my fellow eldest daughters.

Authors Note

Not the Season is short, sweet and spicy and contains some themes that could be upsetting for some readers. Please note the following content warnings:

- Graphic and descriptive sexual scenes, including the use of restraints
- Discussion of a deceased animal (kangaroo) on the side of the road.
- Mentions of body shaming and food shaming. Please take care when reading.

I also want to mention that some of the locations and settings in this book are based on real places, and I have taken some creative liberties when it comes to describing them.

Lastly, I am an Australian author, therefore I have written this book using Australin spelling and grammar.

Thank you, and happy reading!

PART ONE

ONE
Christmas Day
2023

"So Claudia, how's the love life? Locked a man down yet?" my aunty asks from across the table. Twenty minutes into Christmas lunch and the questions have started. Honestly, it's a new record.

"No, Aunty Kathy. If I did, he would probably be here," I say behind the fakest smile.

Concern lines her face. "Well, you better get a move on, lovey. You haven't got much time left, you know."

"I'm well aware of my own body clock, you don't have to worry. If I ever have something to share, I'll share it."

It's a struggle not to roll my eyes and remain pleasant. The same line of questioning, the same concern. I face it at every family get together, and I'm over it. I snapped back once, during a Mother's Day brunch when my bloated stomach was mistaken for a baby bump. The whole family made me feel like a horrible person for speaking up, guilting me even, because of course they are only looking out for me and want me to be happy.

Now look, I love my family. I do. But like a lot of families, they can be a bit overbearing. Intrusive. Misogynistic.

Etcetera. My mum, thankfully, doesn't ask about my love life anymore. I had a slight meltdown after my previous relationship ended last year. Dumped just before Christmas by a man who I thought was my forever person. Mum was there to comfort me, and I told her to please not ask me any more questions about the men in my life. I would tell her when I was ready. She tries to shut down the interrogations from the rest of the family, but they just brush it off as kind curiosity, no harm in asking.

"Yeah, get a move on, Claud. Your baby sister got married before you, surely that's got to sting," my Uncle Ray interrupts from the end of the table.

I look his way and glare. Subtly, of course. "Not at all. I'm so happy she's found someone. I don't compare my life to hers. You shouldn't either really," I say with a nervous lilt.

"I'm just saying—"

"Food's ready!" Mum yells from the kitchen window. I sigh in relief. Conversation temporarily avoided.

My younger sister, Gabi, got married in April this year. I never felt anything but overwhelming joy when she told me. I love her husband Eric and I have no issues with the fact that she got married before me. My family, however, seem to think it's a failure on my part, or something I should be devastated about. Gabi and Eric aren't here for Christmas this year because they're spending it with Eric's family. I'm a little bit jealous.

I make my way into the huge kitchen, where a seafood and Christmas buffet is laid out on the kitchen island. My Aunty Kathy has one of the most beautiful houses – her kitchen looks like it could belong in a magazine. She can't cook to save her life, but she insists on hosting Christmas at her house every year. Thankfully, my mum can cook and always takes care of Christmas lunch. The kitchen is at the back of the house, and bi-fold doors open up to the outdoor deck. Steps lead down to the manicured backyard, complete with a plunge pool. Gabi and I spent most of our summer school holidays here growing up. I love this house.

"What's on the menu today, Mum?" I ask, grabbing a plate.

"We've got prawn cocktail, brown butter seared scallops with pancetta crumb, baked salmon and some oysters, fresh and Kilpatrick," she says, wiping her hands on her apron.

I gag when she mentions oysters.

"You don't have to eat the oysters, don't be so dramatic. I won't be wasting them on you anyway, not after last year."

I tried fresh oysters last Christmas. My thought process was that I'm a proper adult now, with adult taste buds, time to eat adult food. I tried it, gagged for twenty seconds trying to get it down, and ended up spitting it on my plate, looking like something you blow out of your nose when you have the flu.

"Yeah, no thanks. I actually want to enjoy my lunch."

"We've also got the usual. Ham and turkey, pork crackling. Roast spuds and veggie bake."

"Good thing I wore a loose-fitting dress then." My mouth waters, thinking about all the food I'm about to consume.

This is the only thing I like about Christmas. The food. I can always rely on the food getting me through my most hated day of the year. I didn't always hate Christmas. It used to be one of my favourite days. That was until my parents split up when I was eleven years old. Since then, every year I've had to spend Christmas with one side of the family, alternating each year. That was my parents' arrangement, and I felt bad every year, but still tried to enjoy myself. I was the only one of my friends who had two Christmases – lucky me, right? Then I became an adult and had to choose where to spend Christmas each year. And that's when the guilt came in, and the enjoyment was destroyed.

Every year, I have to choose who to disappoint. Every year, I have to have a chat with each parent, determining who to spend the day with. Years of *"Well, it could be Pop's last Christmas"*, *"Gran won't be around much longer"* and *"You spent it with them last year."* Every single year it's the same feeling of dread, and it has ruined any excitement I have for the holiday. Add on top of that a break up on Christmas Eve and… you get the picture.

I want to love Christmas. There is so much to love about it: the lights and the music and seeing families together. Watching little kids' faces light up when they see Santa. I love the idea of Christmas, but I hate the reality of it. Well, my reality anyway.

I chose to spend Christmas with my mum's side of the family this year. This time the decision was based on the weather. It's hot as shit today, and the pool was too good to pass up. I'm spending tomorrow with my dad. He's having the big family Christmas today. Tomorrow will likely consist of the two of us having leftover Christmas ham and cheese toasties on the couch, he'll watch the cricket and I'll be reading.

I pile food onto my plate and make my way back outside. My aunty Kathy looks at the amount of food on my plate and purses her lips. *Do it,* I think to myself. *Make a comment on how much food I'm eating.*

"You're not going to need dinner later if you eat all that, Claud. Are you actually going to finish your plate?"

I bite into a piece of pork crackling with a satisfying crunch and look her directly in the eye. "Yup. With room for dessert too." I take another bite, of ham this time, still keeping eye contact.

"Oh dear," she whispers to herself as she shakes her head.

"Christmas cracker time!" EJ, my teen cousin shouts, waving a Christmas cracker in my face and promptly ending the discussion of my eating habits.

Everyone takes the Christmas cracker in front of them and finds a partner. We all pull the end, and there's shouts of glee when people win and choruses of "oh damn" to those who don't. We share around the paper hats that fall out and take it in turns telling the terrible jokes in between mouthfuls of turkey and potato.

I do indeed finish everything on my plate and avoid the 'concerned' looks from my aunt. After sitting for a while and letting the food digest, I announce that it's time for a swim, and my cousins and I change into our bathers and head down to the pool. As I'm walking past the table, my uncle, who's now a few wines deep, looks me up and down.

"Jeez, girl. Maybe you shouldn't have had that much to eat. You look like you've got a little pot belly brewing there." He laughs, loudly, smacking his hand on his knee as if it's the funniest thing in the world to talk about my body in that way.

"Wow, thanks Uncle Ray." My face turns red. Not from the sun or embarrassment, but from rage and discomfort. How dare he comment on my body. It's so fucking rude, and not to mention downright creepy. He's my *uncle*. So gross. There's always one in the family, and it's times like this I wish I could stand up for myself.

I walk away from my leering uncle and make my way down to the pool, dropping my towel and running to where my cousins are relaxing and tanning in the sun.

"Cannonball!" I yell as I take off into the air and drop into the pool, creating a splash so big it covers both of the girls lying on the pavers. Apparently they're too cool to get into the pool anymore, something about getting their hair wet. Teenagers.

"Claudia!" they both yell in unison, as I come up for air and swipe my hair out of my face.

"What? You looked like you were getting hot." I splash them again for emphasis.

"Ugh, least favourite cousin ever." Bridgit looks over at me, so unimpressed.

"I thought you were cool," Tessa says as she stands, flicking water off her arms.

"I am cool," I whine.

"No, you're not. Cannonball!"

The deep booming voice of my cousin Nath hits me just before the wave does. I choke on water and Tessa and Bridgit shriek and walk away from the pool's edge to escape their older brother. He surfaces, and I splash him in the face.

"Asshole. I thought you were working today."

"I was, but it was quiet in the restaurant and they asked if I wanted to head home early. The air conditioning wasn't working properly, so I wasn't mad about it."

Nath is my favourite cousin. He was born only two months before I was, so we practically grew up together. We act more like brother and sister than cousins, and I'm just as close with him as I am with Gabi.

"Fair enough. What a shame though, I could have used your support during lunch," I say.

"Please tell me it wasn't my parents again," he groans.

"Sorry, it was. Nothing new though, just my dusty old womb, I eat too much, and apparently I should be depressed Gabi got married before me."

"Oh, okay. Sorry Claud, you shouldn't have to deal with that. I know how much you hate coming to these events anyway." He smiles sympathetically, and I kind of hate it.

"It's fine, I'm used to it."

"You shouldn't be though, that's the problem."

"Yeah, I know," I sigh.

We float around on our backs in silence as the twins bicker about who gets the last fairy floss Zooper Dooper. I wonder about how my other side of the family are celebrating today, if it would have been any better to go there instead of here. The all-too-familiar feeling of guilt starts to surface, and I close my eyes and squeeze, trying to block it out.

"Hey, Claud?" Nath asks.

"Yeah?"

"Wanna play mermaids?"

I laugh. We used to play mermaids in this pool all summer long growing up. We'd stay in the pool until we were all pruney, only getting out for food and toilet breaks.

"Fuck yeah, I wanna play mermaids."

We swim and dive and splash around for the next hour or so, until the sun starts to set and I can finally call it a day and drive home. Another Christmas over. Only 364 days until I get to do it all again.

TWO
New Year's Eve
2023

"Babe, if I even attempt to go near my ex tonight at the countdown, please rugby tackle me. I give you permission. Whatever it takes," my best friend, Frankie, says before downing a shot of tequila.

"Or…" I take the bottle away as she tries to pour another shot. "You could just put down the tequila and have the self-control to stay away from him."

"Nah. Where's the fun in that? I want to party!" She snatches the bottle out of my hand and runs away like a naughty toddler caught with a Sharpie.

I turn to Nath, exasperated. "And people wonder why I decided to not drink tonight. Who else would be willing to look after you two idiots?"

"Literally no one, and we love you for it." He pulls me into a headlock and gives me a noogie.

"Ow! Goddamn it, Nath. Get off me, you loser." I shove him off. "Now I have to go fix my hair. And I have to pee. Stay here and behave."

"I can't make any promises, not when the DJ is looking at

me like that," he says as he roams his eyes over the DJ spinning decks in the corner of the living room. I look over and see that the DJ is in fact giving Nath fuck-me eyes. So it begins.

"Okay fine, just be good or whatever. I'll be back in a minute."

I make my way through the crowd in search of the bathroom. Frankie invited us to this house party for New Year's Eve – some friend of a friend, I think. I don't normally do a lot for New Year's, but she really wanted to come, and I didn't want to let her down. It's not the worst party I've ever been to. The house is massive and it has a huge backyard with a pool. They've hired a DJ and there's so much pizza going around, no one will go hungry.

Once we'd arrived, I realised why Frankie wanted to come so badly. Oliver, her on again/off again boyfriend, was here. They are currently off, but I know she was messaging him before Christmas, so it wouldn't surprise me if they were on again after tonight. Oliver isn't a bad guy, he just has severe commitment issues, and Frankie is, well, a hot mess. When they're together, they are magical. When they're apart, they're miserable. I'm sure one day they will grow up and realise they are meant to be, but for now, I console her when they break up and cheer her on when they reunite.

I find the bathroom and try the handle. It's unlocked but I knock just in case.

"Anyone in here?" I ask.

"Occupied!" a muffled voice responds.

"Good thing I checked. The door's unlocked!" I yell through the door.

I hear an "oops" and then the soft click of the lock turning.

I step back into the hallway and lean against the wall, getting my phone out as I wait. I open Instagram but promptly close it when I see photos of happy couples, celebrating at parties and posting cute Christmas photos together. That was me two years ago. Happy and so in love. And then it all fell apart.

Wanting a confidence boost and to shake the image of me and my ex in matching Christmas jammies out of my head, I open a dating app instead. I start swiping, skipping past the usual red flags. Smiling with no teeth? Nope. Wearing sunglasses in every photo? No thanks. Only posting group shots? Who are you, my dude? Drugged up tiger photo in Bali? Get the fuck out. I'm in a rhythm, when suddenly I freeze on a profile. Peter. My ex-boyfriend. Logic tells me to swipe left and move on, but I am just a girl, so of course I click on his profile. His bio is short and to the point, and makes me snort.

"Not looking for anything serious. Peter, you're thirty-six, grow up," I mutter.

Doesn't want kids. Well, at least he's open about that from the start, unlike when he was with me. That's why we broke up. I want kids and have always been vocal about it, while he waited three years before telling me he never wanted to have children. Three years of my life wasted on this man.

The sound of the toilet flushing shakes me out of my stupor and I put my phone back in my pocket. The door opens and I look up, locking eyes with a giant of a man. He's so tall. Baby blues meet my hazel eyes as he looks up and sees me standing against the wall. We stare at each other for a moment, and butterflies flutter low in my belly. He's gorgeous. Dark blonde hair that's slightly messed, as if tussled by fingers, his own or someone else's. A short amount of stubble encompasses his full mouth, which turns up at the corner with a smirk. I break eye contact and clear my throat, opening my mouth to say something to make myself appear less awkward.

"You were in there a while," I blurt out. *Yeah, good one, Claudia. You idiot.*

He looks at me and smiles, a slight blush creeping up his cheeks. "Uh, yeah. Sorry. I think I fell asleep standing up. Jetlag." His voice is low and deep as he runs his fingers through his hair, tussling it even further.

"Oh. Jetlag. Right. That makes sense. I mean, I guess bathrooms are cozy. Not that I hang out in them frequently or anything. I don't. Obviously. That would be weird. I just... you know what, never mind."

I want the ground to swallow me whole.

His lips press into a thin line, like he's trying not to laugh at my rambling. I catch the scent of him, something masculine but also sweet, like shortbread.

"Bathroom is all yours," he says as he walks back towards the rest of the party. It's only when I can't see him that I realise I've been staring at him with my mouth hanging open. I snap my jaw shut and escape into the toilet, praying I can avoid him for the rest of the night.

***

As midnight approaches, I end up losing both Frankie and Nath. I wander around the house looking for them, when I catch Nath making out with the DJ behind the decks. I find Frankie outside, sitting on Oliver's lap, talking to a bunch of people I don't know. She looks over at me and I raise my eyebrow at her. She puts a finger to her lips and shushes me, giggling. I roll my eyes and give Oliver an *I'm watching you* gesture, before blowing a kiss to Frankie as I walk around the rest of the backyard.

I see the bathroom guy standing in a small group, and he locks eyes with me. Nodding slightly, he gives me a wink. I blush but break out into a smile all the same. He turns back to his friends and chuckles at something they're saying.

I look around me and am suddenly overwhelmed with a sense of loneliness, and I need a moment to myself. No one is sitting by the pool so I walk over to it. The heatwave we had here in Adelaide only wanted to stick around over Christmas, it seems. It's a cool 16 degrees tonight, not hot enough to swim, which is why everyone is in the house or under the veranda.

I take my shoes off and sit down on the edge of the pool, dipping my feet in. The water is warmer than I thought it would be.

I check the time and it's 11:50pm. Ten minutes until midnight. I look up at the stars and take a deep breath in. It's probably best that I stay out here for the countdown. I have no one to kiss anyway. I think about Peter, and how last New Year's Eve I spent it on the couch with a tub of ice cream watching *Lord of the Rings*, too heartbroken to even contemplate celebrating. I'm not spending it alone this year, but I am lonely. I see a shooting star dart across the sky, and I close my eyes and make a wish, that this year will bring me everything I've ever wanted. It's ambitious, but you never know.

Footsteps sound on the pavers, forcing me to open my eyes. I look over my shoulder to find Mr. Tall from earlier heading towards the pool, one hand in his pocket and the other typing away on his phone. He looks up and startles when he sees me sitting here alone, almost dropping his phone in the process.

I give a little wave. "Hi," I say.

"Hi. Sorry, I didn't realise you'd come over here. I wasn't following you, I promise," he says with an accent I didn't catch earlier.

"It's all good, I can leave if you want the space," I say, gesturing around me.

"No, no it's fine. I just wanted to… um…"

"Get away from the crowd?" I ask.

"Yeah," he sighs. "Just needed a moment of peace, I guess. You too?"

I nod. He stands there awkwardly for a brief moment, checking the time on his watch before letting out a deep breath.

"Do you mind if I join you?" he asks. "It's almost midnight, and I don't really want to deal with all of that." He hikes his thumb over his shoulder at the rest of the party, who are starting to gather inside near the DJ for the countdown.

I huff a laugh, because I feel the same. "Yeah, that's fine. That's why I'm here too. The water's warm enough, if you want to put your feet in."

He kicks off his shoes to sit beside me, tentatively putting a toe in the water before going all in, like he didn't believe me that it was warm. He leans back on his hands and closes his eyes, taking in a deep breath before looking over at me and holding out a hand for me to shake.

"I'm Henry, by the way."

"I'm Claudia." I reach out and shake his hand. "Nice to meet you."

"Likewise. Do you know many people here tonight?" he asks.

"Not many. My best friend dragged me along, my cousin too. What about you?"

"Just my roommate. I've only been here a few days and he thought it might be nice for me to party like the Australian's do." He chuckles.

"Oh really? Where are you from?"

"Guess." He smirks.

His accent is strong, and my go to would be to say he's from the US, but something tells me that's not right. He's too polite.

"Canada?"

He blinks. "Yeah, Ontario, to be more specific. Most people guess America, nice work." He smiles again, and my lips twitch up at the corners as well.

"Thanks. That's pretty cool though. So when you say you've only been here for a few days, do you mean Adelaide?"

"Australia. I arrived on the twenty-ninth. Hence the jetlag and falling asleep in the bathroom."

I laugh. "Oh wow, okay that makes more sense now. What brings you here?"

"Something new, mostly. I've always wanted to come here. I had planned to travel in 2020 but then the pandemic happened and, well, you know the rest."

"That I do. So how long are you staying?"

"I don't know yet. I'm planning on at least a year or two. And then I'll see what happens."

"Nice. Sounds like an adventure."

"I hope so."

We sit in silence for a few moments, swishing our feet in the water. I check my phone, only three minutes until midnight.

"It's 11:57," I tell him.

"Almost midnight."

"Yep."

He clears his throat. "So, do you have a partner?"

I laugh. "Nope. No boyfriend, no husband, nothing. You?"

"Nah. Just me, myself and I." He runs his fingers through his hair again, and I find myself wanting it to be my fingers instead. "No one to kiss at midnight?"

I glance sideways at him and he's looking at me, his blue eyes piercing mine. I swallow, hard, and my eyes dip to his mouth.

"No, no one to kiss at midnight," I say quietly.

He smiles a little, and my heart rate picks up. I think he's hinting at something, something I think I might want, but in true Claudia style I don't know what to do, so I choose my safest option. Escape.

"Well, I guess I better go and join the rest of the group. It was nice meeting you!" I push myself up off of the edge of the pool to stand.

"Oh, okay. I should—"

As I go to step away, I trip over myself and yelp as I fall sideways, straight into the pool with a splash. The water may have been a nice temperature on the surface but underneath, it's cold. Breaking the surface of the water with a splutter, I push my wet hair out of my eyes. I turn to look up at Henry, who is now standing and covering his mouth with his hand to stop himself from laughing.

"Well, that's embarrassing," I say.

"Are you okay?" he asks.

"I'm not injured, if that's what you're asking."

His shoulders are shaking with laughter, as someone yells out to everyone left outside that there's one more minute until midnight.

"Great," I mutter.

He glances back to the rest of the party and then looks down at me. Smiling brightly, I have a second to close my eyes as he jumps into the pool next to me, covering me with water once again. He surfaces and laughs, throwing his head back.

"Uh, question. Why did you do that?" I ask, giving him a little splash.

"So you aren't alone," he says with a soft smile, and my heart melts a little. I smile back at him.

"Thirty seconds until midnight!"

Our heads turn towards the house and we realise that no one else is left outside. It's just us. I can sense him looking at me, and I turn my head back, slowly. Somehow, we've drifted closer to each other, so close our legs keep bumping as I tread the water.

"Ten, nine, eight..."

"Claudia?"

I drift even closer.

"...seven, six..."

"Yeah?" I say as our breaths mingle.

"...five, four..."

"Can I kiss you?"

"...three, two..."

"Yes."

"...one, Happy New Year!"

Henry places one hand on the back of my head and pulls me into him, our mouths colliding. He's gentle at first, his lips soft on mine. Our bodies press up against each other, and I wrap my legs around his waist. Backing us up against the edge of the pool, he deepens the kiss. His tongue sweeps over mine and something within me ignites. Suddenly, I can't get enough. His hands explore my body under the water and I grind my hips against him.

I don't know how long we make out for, but eventually the kiss slows. I rest my forehead against his and close my eyes, catching my breath and calming my racing heart. I pull back to look at him and smile, almost painfully. He smiles back, and then, I'm laughing. He joins in, and we start splashing around, grabbing at each other in the water, kissing when we can. I feel giddy, and it's only when my teeth start clattering that we decide we should probably get out of the pool.

We wring out our clothes as much as we can. I'm wearing a dress and squeeze water from the skirt. Henry, however, pulls his shirt off over his head and twists it, water dripping out all over the pavers. My thighs squeeze together involuntarily at the sight of him partially naked. His arms are thick with muscle, and his body is well taken care of. A smattering of hair trails down from his belly button and into his shorts, and I find myself fantasising about where it leads to…

"Committing me to memory?" he asks.

I tear my eyes away from his pants and look up to find him smirking at me. "Yes, actually. I like what I see." It's the most confident I've felt all night.

His smile broadens and he tucks a wet curl behind my ear, not that it will do much to stop me looking like a drowned rat. "I hope you haven't ruined your dress. It's real pretty."

I look down at the sundress I'm wearing, now clinging to my body like a second skin. My nipples are poking through, and I know he notices because his finger trails across my collarbone and down my sternum. He traces a line under my left breast and I gasp at the touch.

I lean into him again, wanting him to kiss me, when we are rudely interrupted.

"Oh my god, Claudia! What happened to you?" Frankie squeals.

"Um… we fell in the pool," I say, pointing to Henry and taking a small step back, putting some distance between us. "Does anyone know where we could get a towel?"

A woman I don't know runs inside and brings out two towels

for us, and I wrap one around myself, hoping to keep the chill at bay. Frankie pulls me aside, concern lining her face. Or it could be elation – she's pretty drunk so I can't really tell.

"Claud, who is that guy and why did you both fall in the pool?"

I giggle, and she gasps dramatically. "His name is Henry, and he's Canadian. He was my New Year's kiss," I whisper-scream.

She bounces on her feet and claps her hands. "Oh my god! This is amazing! So are you going to go home with him?" she asks, poking me in the stomach.

"I don't know. I'm trying to not do one night stands anymore. Plus, I'm sober and I don't know if he's been drinking. Plus, he fell asleep standing up earlier…"

"Huh?"

"Jetlag, apparently." I wave a hand. "Either way, I don't think I will tonight. Instead… I'll get his number, maybe go on a date."

"Ooo, you like this guy."

"Okay, I barely know him, let's not get carried away with ourselves. He's nice. And hot. And a good kisser." I sigh.

Frankie makes kissy faces at me and I swat her away. We go back to the group, and I gesture to Henry to follow me down the side of the house.

"So, I think I'm going to go home, I need a hot shower, like now." I laugh.

"Not the worst idea," he says, laughing with me.

"Do you need a lift or anything? I didn't drink tonight, so you'd be safe with me."

"Oh… um…" He checks the time on his phone. "Yeah, actually, I will. If you don't mind?"

"It's no problem. I'll just go and say goodbye to Frankie and Nath."

I tell Frankie I'm leaving and taking Henry home, and she winks at me and nudges me with her elbow. Walking away, I go in search of Nath. I find out he's locked away somewhere with the DJ, so I send him a quick message telling him I've gone home.

I meet Henry at the front of the house and he gives me his address, which, funnily enough, is only two suburbs over from where I live, and on the way. We spend most of the car ride in comfortable silence, listening to the RnB songs playing on the radio. As we stop at a traffic light, he reaches over and takes my hand in his. I look out of the window to my right to stop him from seeing the ridiculous grin that spreads across my face.

I pull up at the front of his house, and of course it gets a little awkward. I don't know what to do so I fidget with the towel that's still wrapped around me.

"So, would it be okay if I got your number and gave you a call sometime?" he asks, and I whip up my head to look at him.

"I was going to ask for your number. You beat me to it."

We smile at each other and swap phones, entering our numbers. I call his, just to make sure it's not fake – I didn't think it would be, but I relax when I hear the ringtone.

"Well, it was great meeting you," I say. "Thank you for being my New Year's kiss."

"It was a pleasure. You made my night worthwhile. I won't be forgetting it in a hurry." He leans over the centre console and I kiss him again, the same intense feeling taking over me like it did in the pool. Slowly, we pull apart, and looking into his eyes in that moment, I feel like this could definitely be the start of something new and wonderful. He doesn't ask me to come in, or even hint at us taking this further, and I respect the hell out of him for it.

"Thanks for driving me. Can you message me when you get home, so I know you're safe?" He kisses my knuckles, and I swoon.

"I live ten minutes from here," I whisper.

"Ten minutes, one hundred minutes, it doesn't matter. I want to know. Happy New Year," he says, laying one final kiss on the top of my hand.

"Happy New Year, Henry."

He gets out of the car and I watch him walk into his house. Driving home, I'm on cloud nine and do, indeed, text him when I get home safe.

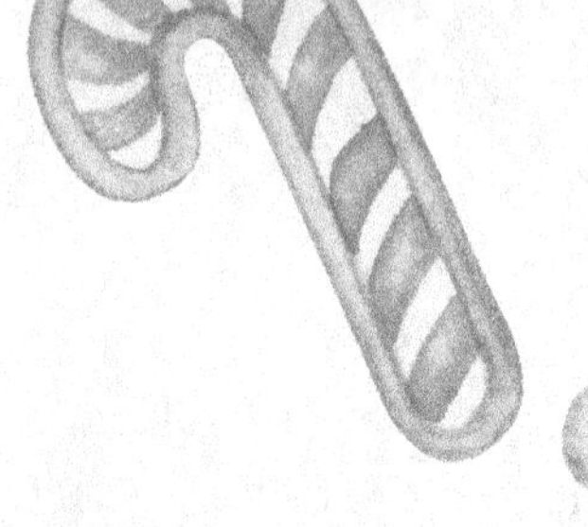

THREE
First Date

"I'm not nervous, you're nervous. Shut up," I mumble under my breath.

"Oh babe, I am definitely nervous. I know what you're like on dates. The first sign of an ick and you immediately run away," Frankie says.

It's the first Saturday of the month, and for us, that means manicures. Usually we would go for a beach walk afterwards. However, today I'm skipping the walk because Henry has asked me out on a date. Less than twenty-four hours after we'd met and made out in the pool, he was texting me. Another twenty-four hours after that and he asked me out. We're meeting for a coffee, and I'm absolutely shitting myself over the idea of a date. He's been so sweet, and we've already made out, so I don't really have a reason to say no. Other than my general distrust in men, of course.

"Well, obviously. I won't settle for any red flags," I tell her.

"You walked out on a date because the guy said he didn't like pizza."

"Yes, and? I'm sorry, but I can't trust a man who doesn't like pizza. Who doesn't like pizza? And what else don't they like? Puppies? Sunsets? Foreplay? No thanks."

She laughs. I have been picky with my dates lately, and I have no issues with ending a date early if it isn't going well. Admittedly though, I didn't just end the date with the guy because of the pizza thing. I didn't tell Frankie this, but as I was walking back to the table from the restaurant bathroom, I saw him open a message that was very clearly a nude photo. He was on a date with me and receiving nudes from someone else. I didn't tell her, because I felt like it was my fault somehow. I wasn't interesting enough, or hot enough, or good enough, to keep him entertained for one dinner date. It made me feel awful, so I told her only about the pizza, to keep things light-hearted.

"Just promise me you'll give this guy a chance. There is clearly a connection between the two of you, otherwise you wouldn't have let him stick his tongue in your mouth at New Year's."

"True," I mutter. "He does actually seem somewhat decent. He holds a conversation well, doesn't leave me on read. Actually, I think he's been the one to initiate every conversation we've had." I crinkle my brows in realisation. "I guess it's a good sign that I'm not trying to think of an excuse not to go, which is my usual pre-date routine."

"Exactly. Who knows, he might just be the one to bring back your faith in men!" She beams, hopeful.

"Maybe."

"So, what are you going to talk about on this date?" she asks.

"Life goals, five-year plan, stance on marriage and children, how he feels about pizza... the usual."

"Ha!" she snorts.

I smile back at her, but her expression turns somewhat serious.

"Wait, are you really going to ask him about marriage and babies? On the first date?"

I shrug. "Of course. I'm not investing any more time in men

who don't know what they want out of a relationship. Especially when they're in their thirties. I wasted three years on Peter and I refuse to do that again."

She winces at that. "Yeah, I know. I get it."

"And honestly, a true man shouldn't be afraid of questions like that. Isn't it better to be on the same page with the same goals early, rather than find out later on when you're already invested?"

Thinking about what happened with Peter has my heart pounding rapidly with hurt and frustration. Three years, all of those prime years, wasted. And it was all because I'd had it drilled into me that it's not a good idea to ask those sorts of questions too early in a relationship. You don't want to come on too strong, people told me. So I held back, I went with the flow, I waited until we'd moved in together and were solid enough to ask. All to be told his dreams did not match mine at all. So now I ask the questions straight up. So far, every man has given me a half-arsed answer or refused to comment. One guy joked about putting a baby in me that very night. My drink accidentally-on-purpose ended up all over his shirt and I left immediately.

"She makes a good point," my nail technician says with a nod.

"Thank you, Ash! You get me." This woman has been doing my nails for years and has heard every detail about my love life. She probably knows me just as well as Frankie does. I love her.

"Oh don't get me wrong, I definitely agree," says Frankie. "Let's hope Henry is open and honest. He's cute, and you need a good man in your life. And you need to have sex."

"Frankie!"

"You know I'm right." She winks.

She is right. It has been a while, and the kiss that Henry and I shared ignited a need within me that I hadn't felt in a very long time.

"Can we talk about something else, please? What's the latest with you and Oliver?" I ask. We haven't had a proper debrief since the party, and all I know is they went home together.

"No comment."

"Francesca," I groan.

"Ugh. Fine. I went back to his house after the party and we… rekindled. So to speak."

"Well, I mean that was obvious. You were in his lap for most of the night. I meant what's happening now? Are you talking?"

Oliver has a habit of doing this: getting her back in his bed and then ghosting her again. He drives me insane, and I hate seeing Frankie being messed around, but she loves him so much and so I stand by her and support her where I can. I use Nath to debrief – at least he's on the same page as me.

"We are. More than ever, actually. He hasn't left me alone since the party." Her eyebrows knit together in thought. "I'm hopeful, but I am cautious. I don't want to get my hopes up. Again." She sighs.

"Well, I'm here to support you, whichever way it goes. I hope this time he has his shit sorted."

"Me too."

***

After my nail date with Frankie, I rush home to get ready for my date with Henry. Not that I have much to do to prepare – I don't put in a lot of effort for first dates appearance-wise. Why spend the time getting myself dolled up for a man who will most likely waste my time? Though, the thought of seeing Henry again *almost* makes me want to put in more effort, but I stand strong. After all, he wanted to kiss me when I was sopping wet and fully clothed, I'm sure I don't need to try too hard with him. I don a simple white shirt dress and sandals, chuck on a bit of mascara, brush out the loose waves of my short dark hair, and I'm ready.

I get in my car and as I'm driving, the nervousness kicks in. What if he was actually just really drunk at the party and isn't actually that into me? I hyper-fixate on this until I pull up to the café, and by the time I walk in I'm convinced he's going to take one look at me and leave. I look around the space, and spot him sitting at a small table by the window. He looks over at me, and as our eyes meet, he smiles so brightly I almost have to look away. Negative thoughts, gone. I smile coyly back at him and suddenly feel incredibly shy. I walk over to the table, and he stands to greet me, leaning in to kiss me on the cheek, like a gentleman.

"Claudia, lovely to see you again," he says.

"Hi, Henry," I say, in a tone slightly above a whisper. I forgot just how spell-bindingly attractive he is, not to mention the accent. And his height. *Oof.* I'm in danger.

"This is for you." He pulls out a single white rose and holds it out to me.

"For me?" I ask, taking it from him as I blink, slowly, like I can't believe a man has brought me a flower on a first date.

"Yeah. I know it's super cheesy, but I couldn't help myself." He gestures for me to sit at the table, and as I do, I breathe in the soft rosy scent.

"Thank you," I say gently. "It's beautiful."

My inner girly girl is screaming right now because this is not normal dating etiquette. Is it because he's Canadian? Have Australian men really dropped the ball with dating so bad, that I want to squeal over a single rose?

"You're welcome." He smiles again.

Fully taking in my surroundings, I find that the café is actually more of a bakery. Fresh bread lines the shelves behind the counter and pastries fill the cabinets. The furniture is a soft dusty blue, with pops of cream accents. Vines are draped along the walls, and each white table has a small bouquet of daisies. It has a vintage charm and an overall calming effect. It's sweet, perfect for a first date.

"This place is beautiful, I can't believe I've never been here before," I tell him. It's only five minutes from my house.

"I love it here. They make the best chocolate croissants."

"Well, I guess I'll have to try one."

"Great idea. So, how have you been since I saw you last?"

Since I saw him last… when we made out in the pool and I immediately developed a crush.

"Fine," I tell him. "Just enjoying my school holidays. Reading and baking, going to the beach."

"School holidays?"

I nod.

"Yeah, Miss Michaels is my name. I'm a PE teacher at a primary school. I get five weeks off over the summer."

"That's cool. And you like baking?" he asks.

"I love it. I'm not the greatest baker in the world, but I find it calming. I love making cookies mostly. Do you like baking?"

"You could say that…" he trails off, just as one of the staff approach us to take our order.

"Henry, Henry, even on your day off you can't keep away, huh?" the older woman tuts.

I look at Henry, then to the woman, and then back to him. "You work here?" I ask.

"I do. I'm their new baker." He beams.

"Best baker going around, in my opinion," she says. "And who is this lovely young lady that you've brought in today, Henry?"

"This is Claudia. Claudia, meet Shelly. The best boss I've ever had." He smiles affectionately at Shelly, and my heart melts a little.

"Nice to meet you. Your shop is beautiful," I tell her.

"Thank you, darling, she's my pride and joy. How long have you known my dear Henry?"

"Not long!" I jump in before he can say anything. "We met at a party on New Year's Eve and this is our first time catching up since."

"Oh so this is a first date then! How exciting! Well, I won't take up too much of your time. What can I get for you both?" She pulls out a note pad and pen from her apron.

"An iced dirty chai latte please, and a chocolate croissant," I say, looking at Henry.

"Oh Henry baked those fresh last night!"

I laugh. "No wonder you told me they make the best croissants. You make them."

"Guilty," he says, raising his hand. "I'll have an English breakfast tea, and a chocolate croissant as well. Thank you, Shelly."

"No problemo. You kids have fun now!"

She walks away and I make a mental note to come back here as often as possible.

"She's lovely," I tell him.

"She really is. I had no idea how I was going to find a job when I first got here. I came in on the day I landed, desperate for some carbs, and we got talking. Her baker had just quit and she was about to start advertising. I told her I was a baker back home and she threw an apron at me, told me to prove it. I baked her a cake and she hired me on the spot."

"Incredible. Did you work somewhere similar back in Canada?" I ask.

"My family own a bakery, has done for a few generations now. It's the Cambell family legacy. I'm from a town called Almonte, in Ontario," he tells me. "I was helping my family in the kitchen the moment I was old enough to hold a spoon. The plan is for me to take over the business once my parents retire, but I wanted to travel first. Australia has always been on my bucket list. I'm actually a dual citizen; my dad was born in Sydney. He moved to Canada when he was twenty, met my mum, fell in love with her and the town, and never left."

"Wow, that's amazing. I have to admit, I've never heard of Almonte. Tell me about it."

Our food and drinks arrive and I dig in, listening to him describe his home town.

"It's located along the Mississippi River, so there's a lot to see and do. It's a small-ish town, and the people are so friendly and welcoming. It holds a certain charm to it that makes everyone feel like they're home. I've never lived anywhere else until now. Adelaide gives me a similar vibe actually. The people have been so kind."

"It sounds wonderful."

"It is. My favourite time of year in Almonte is Christmas. The entire town lights up with Christmas lights and festivals and markets. The snow falls and it's just... magical."

"Magical. Can't say I've experienced a magical Christmas, not since I was a child anyway."

His shoulders slump. "Do you not like Christmas?" he asks.

"I dread it. It's been a long time since I've felt the joy and wonder of Christmas. I love the idea of it, but the reality is, it's my least favourite holiday."

"Is there any reason why?"

"Yes, but I'd rather not trauma dump on you on a first date." I laugh and he smiles.

"Okay. You can tell me about it when you're ready. Let's change the topic."

"Thank you."

"What do you want to talk about?" he asks.

"I want to get to know you."

"Okay, shoot."

"Well, I tend to cut right to the chase with first dates. But you actually seem nice, so I don't want to come across too blunt."

"No, please, cut to the chase. What do you want to know?" He leans back in his chair, teacup in hand.

"Are you looking for something casual or something serious? Because I won't lie, I'm not really in the market for a casual fling right now." I'm wringing my hands under the table, nervous as to what he's going to say.

"Straight to the point, I like it. I wasn't planning on looking for anything serious, I'll be honest with you."

My shoulders slump.

"However," he starts, "I am open to the possibility of a relationship, with the right person. But I am only here temporarily, maybe for two years, and then I plan to move back home."

"Yeah, that makes sense," I say, slightly deflated.

"I will say though, I wasn't expecting to meet someone so soon after moving here. I can't deny that I am drawn to you, and I want to get to know you. I haven't stopped thinking about that kiss at the party." He stares at my mouth, and my stomach does a backflip.

"I can't stop thinking about it either," I tell him. "I want to get to know you too. But you don't plan on being here long term, and that isn't exactly comforting."

"I know." He takes my hand and rubs his thumb across my knuckles, eliciting a shiver to run down my spine. "Honestly, I can't predict what the future will hold for me. I haven't been here very long, but I already love it. I could see myself staying, but I'd be leaving my family and the future I had envisioned behind. It'd have to take something or someone pretty special to make me stay."

"That's understandable," I say, taking my hand back from his. "How do you feel about marriage, and do you want children?" I blurt out.

He doesn't flinch or scoff at the question like I expect. "I'd love to get married. And I definitely want kids. At least two."

I blink. "Really?"

"Yeah, I've always wanted kids. I can't wait to have a family of my own," he says sincerely.

"Wow. I think you're the first man I've ever dated to answer that question so honestly and so quickly."

He shrugs. "No point lying about it. I actually appreciate the question. Most people are too scared to ask those types of questions straight up."

"Tell me about it," I mumble. Another question pops into my mind. "Do you like pizza?"

"Duh. Who doesn't like pizza? That's just weird. If you don't like pizza, you don't like happiness." He scoffs.

"Exactly!" I laugh. He smiles at me, happy to hear he gave the right answer.

"So, what are you looking for then?" he asks me.

"Someone to settle down with. Someone I can be myself around. Someone who wants the same things in life. I'm happy in my job, but everything else in life I feel like I've come up short. My family love to remind me of it too."

He says nothing but cocks his head, looking at me so intently that I almost start squirming in my chair.

"Sorry, I don't know where that all came from. I'm not normally so open on a first date."

He nods, a small smile playing on his lips. "It seems that perhaps we are very comfortable around each other."

"So it does."

We end up sitting and talking for another two hours. Shelly keeps refilling our drinks and dropping off little sweet treats onto the table, all made by Henry of course. The conversation is easy and he answers every question I throw at him, no matter how obscure or forward. He takes my hand in his again and only lets it go to drink or eat. I don't know if it's his baby blue eyes, his bright smile or the way the deep timbre of his voice puts me at ease, but I've never felt so comfortable with a man so quickly.

At the end of the date, he walks me to my car, and just like he did at the party, he asks if he can kiss me. I grin stupidly and nod, so he leans down and kisses me. It's nothing like our kiss in the pool; it's soft and sweet. A promise of gentleness and patience. A promise of something more to come.

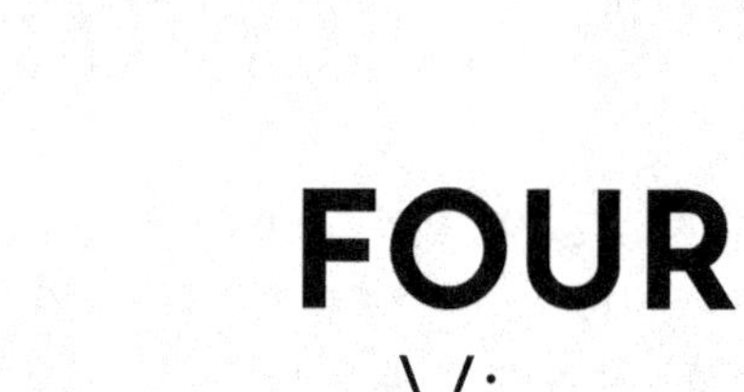

FOUR
Vino

The days go by, and not a single one passes where I don't see or hear from Henry. Without fail, he sends me a message every morning when he leaves for work, so that when I wake up, I wake to a text. It's not always a good morning message either – sometimes it's a funny video or a meme, sometimes it's a cute photo, sometimes it's… not a cute photo. Last week I sat upright in bed when I opened the message he had sent. There he stood, shirtless in the bakery, wearing nothing but an apron and coated in flour. His perfect body on full display. The caption read: *Oops, I got a little bit messy this morning*. It made me chuckle, and super horny.

We haven't slept together yet, despite our ever-growing attraction. I told him straight up that I will not jump into bed with anyone again until I'm sure they aren't going to waste my time. He agreed, and so we've waited. He's come over to my house a few times, and a few hot and steamy make out sessions have ensued. The tension is building, and after seeing that photo of him, I know I need to have him soon.

Our second date happened a few weeks ago. We spent the afternoon lazing on the beach, eating fresh fruit and ice cream, getting to know each other on a deeper level. I took him to Port Willunga, one of the southern beaches in Adelaide, known for its crystal blue waters and soft white sand. Golden cliffs surround the beach, with hidden caves and rock pools scattered throughout. Henry had heard about Australian beaches and was fully prepared to be bombarded with huge waves and blue bottle jellyfish, but what he found was the complete opposite.

The beaches of Adelaide are calm and flat, perfect for swimming, floating, or playing a game of catch. Whilst it is fun to jump in the big waves at the beach, I prefer the smaller waves – it makes the whole experience a lot more relaxing. It was a perfect day, until the shark plane flew overhead and set off the alarm. Henry ran out of the water so fast I nearly tripped over from laughing. Reports later said that a small shark was spotted about a kilometre off shore, but it was close enough that Henry decided he would be staying on dry land for the rest of the afternoon.

As we munched on fish and chips for dinner, we planned our third date. Henry loves wine, and hasn't yet been to the Barossa Valley, so I declared we go on a mini wine tour. I was given a voucher for my birthday last year for a private driver and an afternoon of wine tastings. I had planned on going with Frankie, but I knew she wouldn't mind me using it for a date with Henry, so I cashed it in and booked it for the last Saturday in February, which is today.

The weather is perfect for a wine tasting. It's 32 degrees and sunny. I'm wearing a sage green and white gingham jumpsuit, with strappy heels and a boater hat to keep the sun off my face. Henry shows up to my house wearing white shorts, a navy linen shirt and leather sneakers. He's looking tan, and his dark blonde hair looks a little lighter after spending only a few months in the Australian sun. His blue eyes shine in the daylight, and I'm mesmerised.

"White shorts on a wine tour? You're brave." I laugh as I greet him with a kiss.

"Do you think I should go back and change?" he asks. "These are the nicest shorts I own, and I didn't think denim cutoffs would work."

"Nah. You look amazing. Just don't be sad if you end up with wine all over them."

"It's just the two of us, I'm sure it'll be fine."

Yeah, that's what everyone says right before they go on a wine tour.

"The driver will be here any minute. Are you ready?" I ask.

"I am. I'm very excited. How many wineries are we going to?"

"Three. Jacob's Creek, Rockford Wines and Kellermeister. A couple of my favourites."

Our driver pulls up in a sleek black car and introduces himself. His name is Jeremy, and according to him, he is the best private driver and self-certified wine expert in all of Adelaide. He's polite and has a delightful sense of humour, and we are soon on our way.

Jacob's Creek is our first stop. We arrive just after the lunch rush and are greeted warmly by one of the staff, who takes us on a walk through the vineyards to give us a quick rundown of the history of the winery. It's 170 years old and one of the most well-known Barossa wineries around the world. After the vineyard tour, we treat ourselves to an afternoon picnic, complete with a bottle of wine and a charcuterie board of locally-made produce.

Henry has brought along a disposable camera to capture the memories of this date, and I catch him not so subtly taking a candid photo of me as I sip on a glass of Pinot Gris.

"You look so beautiful in this light," he tells me, and a blush rushes to my cheeks.

I smile shyly. "Thank you."

I'm still not used to receiving outright compliments from him. I used to have to beg for any sort of affection or adoration from Peter, but Henry seems to give it out in spades without even having to be prompted. Once again, I am shocked at my being impressed by the absolute bare minimum, but grateful to have found a man who so openly says how he feels.

After our picnic, we get back into the car and drive a short distance to Rockford Wines. This is one of my favourite wineries and I just had to include it on the list. The old stone buildings give a rustic farmhouse feel, and the wine is so crisp and delicious. It's a lot busier here, so we don't get to do a full tasting experience, deciding instead to buy another bottle and sit outside to enjoy more of the sunshine.

"So I have to ask, how are you feeling about everything?" Henry says.

"Everything, as in the wine?" I ask.

"No, I mean about us."

"Oh. Um…"

"Sorry to put you on the spot," he laughs. "Must be the wine giving me the audacity."

"No, it's fine," I reassure him. "I guess I'm feeling… good. Really good. But also, nervous and a little hesitant."

"Because of my whole *I'm only here for two years* situation?"

"Yeah. I fear I may have some abandonment issues. And so, to be dating someone who isn't even a permanent resident… it sets off the nervous system a little bit." I laugh, and he chuckles in return.

"Yeah, I'm sorry for making your life more complicated."

"Don't be sorry. Despite its complications, I'm really enjoying getting to know you. You're probably the nicest guy I've ever dated," I tell him.

"Can I ask about your dating history? You don't have to tell me if you don't feel comfortable."

"You first," I say.

"Okay. Well, sadly there isn't much to tell. I've had a few girlfriends over the years, though I don't know if I'd label them as anything serious. My longest relationship lasted two years, and that ended three years ago. We nearly lost the bakery because of Covid, and so once life started looking normal again, I had to put everything into getting business back up and running. Unfortunately, my focus on work caused tension and resentment. I didn't give her the attention and dedication she deserved and it drove us apart. Since then, I focussed on the business and moved back in with my parents to save money to come to Australia. I haven't dated anyone since that relationship ended."

I nod, impressed by his own self-awareness and accountability for his wrongdoings in his relationships. It's so healthy and refreshing, and it makes me feel comfortable enough to share my story. So I tell him everything.

I tell him how Peter was a few years older than me and we worked together at the same school. He was a maths teacher; I was a newly employed PE teacher. We flirted back and forth at work a lot, and then one day when I was scrolling through a dating app I came across his profile. I'd had a few wines, so I swiped right, and we matched. He messaged me almost instantly, and the flirty banter from work turned into something a little more heated. We hooked up that weekend, and the weekend after that, and the one after that. Eventually he asked me out on a real date, and then after six months, I asked him what we were. He said whatever I wanted us to be, and so that's how he became my boyfriend. Not the most romantic of propositions, but I was smitten and happy that we were finally official.

We dated for three years, and a lot of the time it was great. We travelled, spent time with each other's families, and eventually, moved in together. We had started to create what I thought was my dream life. Not once during that time did I ever ask if he wanted children, or to get married. I just assumed he did, because I was so vocal about wanting kids and dreaming about my wedding day. Why would he be with me if he didn't want the same things?

Then, two years into the relationship, Gabi announced that she was engaged to Eric. I was so happy and excited for her, I spent the whole day dancing around the house giddy with excitement. Peter laughed at me and said, *"Don't you be getting any ideas now,"* and I just stood there in confusion. I asked him what he meant about that, and he said to not expect a ring from him anytime soon. I thought he meant because we'd only been dating for two years, so I brushed it aside as an off-the-cuff comment.

Gabi and Eric had a short engagement and were married nine months later in November. It was a beautiful day, and I was riding on the high for weeks. One day I asked Peter if we were to get married, where would he want do it. He looked at me and told me he doesn't plan on ever getting married. I laughed at first because I though he was joking. He wasn't. He said he thought I knew that, to which I promptly told him that I absolutely did not know. He apologised for misleading me, and a part of me thought it was okay, that maybe I didn't need to get married. A lot of couples don't get married and live long and happy lives together.

I didn't say anything for a while, but I couldn't let it go, and so on Christmas Eve as I was wrapping up the last of the presents, I brought it up again. He told me again he had absolutely no interest in marriage. Then, as I held my breath, I asked about children. His response? *"Absolutely not."* I still remember the shock wave that cursed through my body as he said those two words. I completely lost the plot. I'm not someone who yells at anyone – I don't even yell in the classroom or during sports games – but I yelled at him that night.

I asked how he could possibly date me for three years, knowing that I wanted children at the very least, and not say anything. He told me he'd just hoped that after a while I would forget about it or change my mind. Then, with tears streaming down my face and Christmas carols playing in the background, he said if I wanted those things so badly then he would make it easier on me by ending the relationship, so I could go and find someone else who did. In one ten-minute conversation, my life was turned upside down.

The house was leased in my name, so I demanded that he leave. He packed a bag, told me he was sorry, and left. I spent the rest of Christmas Eve sobbing into my pillow, and then spent Christmas Day putting on a brave face in front of everyone when I told them that we had broken up but I was totally fine.

At some point during my story, Henry takes a hold of my hand and rubs his thumb in comforting circles.

"Wow. What a total dick."

"Yeah," I huff out with a laugh.

"Now I know why you were so upfront about the marriage and kids question on our first date."

"I've asked about it on every first date I've been on since. I just… I don't want to waste any more time on someone who doesn't want the same things as I do. So when you answered honestly, and our goals aligned, I felt safe," I admit.

"I can hand on my heart tell you that I wouldn't be here with you now if I wasn't interested in seeing where this goes."

"I believe you. I wouldn't be here if I didn't think you were going to screw me over."

We don't bring up his current two-year plan, and I hope it's because he has the same thought as me. Neither of us know what the future will bring, and so maybe we should try and embrace what this is. He leans in and kisses me, his lips are soft and sweet, tasting like the wine we've been drinking. I grab a hold of his collar and deepen the kiss. I'm feeling flushed from the Pinot, and a pleasant buzz has started forming in my head, loosening my inhibitions just a smidge. My tongue sweeps over his, and he lets out a small sigh.

"Claudia, we are in public," he mutters against my lips, not breaking the kiss even for a moment.

"Maybe I don't care."

He laughs and I pull back to look into his eyes. Eyes that hold so much honesty, adoration and a spark of something we are yet to explore. I look down and swirl my wine glass, avoiding eye contact for what I'm about to say, suddenly nervous.

"Just so you know..." I pause. "I'm not seeing or talking to anyone but you, and I'm not really interested in seeing or talking to anyone else either."

He tilts my chin up so that he's looking me in the eyes once more. "I'm not interested in anyone else either," he says.

"Okay."

"Okay."

We smile at each other, and he taps me on the tip of my nose, causing me to scrunch my face up and swat him away.

"Come on, lets finish this bottle so we can head to the last winery. I think you'll like this one. We might, if you're lucky, see some kangaroos."

"Kangaroos?" he shouts and promptly drinks the rest of his wine in one gulp.

"Calm your farm, I can't drink wine as fast as you can. We have plenty of time. Plus, I said we *might* see a kangaroo. Don't get too excited in case there aren't any." I chuckle at his eagerness to see an animal that I see so frequently that I don't think twice about it.

I sit and finish my wine, taking my sweet time to the point where Henry is almost begging me to drink faster. He drags me to the car, and demands Jeremy drive us as fast as we can to Kellermeister Wines. Jeremy follows the speed limit because he's a good driver, but we arrive within fifteen minutes anyway. This winery is the least busy of the three, and so we are offered another tour of the vineyard before we settle in for our final tasting.

As we make our way down the rows and rows of lush green vines, Henry suddenly stops dead in front of me, causing me to walk straight into his back, almost tripping over. I look around him to see why he's stopped, and I'm not surprised when I see two kangaroos nibbling on the grass about ten metres ahead of us.

"Oh my god. They're real," Henry breathes.

I look at our host and she looks back at me confused. I laugh and shake my head, wrapping an arm around Henry's waist.

"Never mind him," I tell her. "He's from Canada and has never seen one before."

"They're so cute!" he squeaks. "This is a bucket list moment for sure."

"Really? They're so normal to me. I don't even blink half the time I see them anymore." I try and think of a Canadian animal that might make me feel the same way. "I guess I'd probably have the same reaction if I saw a squirrel or a beaver. They don't seem real to me."

"This is so cool. Can I get closer?" he asks, not even listening to me.

"You can try. These two hang around the vineyard most days and are pretty used to people," says our host. "When you are done playing tourist, come back into the cellar door and I'll get you sorted with a drink."

I thank her, and Henry and I slowly creep closer to the kangaroos. Their grey fur appears super soft in the late afternoon sun, and their tall ears twitch and flutter in anticipation with every step we take. The smaller one pops her head up when we're about five metres away and looks at us curiously, the larger one joining her shortly after. I make a kissing noise, and one of them hops closer to us. Henry squats down so they aren't as intimidated by his size and reaches out a hand. The larger one hops closer and closer to us, until it's sniffing Henry's hand. He gasps and stays perfectly still, as I quickly take out my phone and take some photos. He is smiling ear to ear, and I'm so happy I'm the one to give him this experience, even if it does seem so simple to me. Suddenly, the roos must hear something in the distance because they quickly turn their heads away from us and bounce away through the grapevines.

Henry stands and swoops me up into his arms and gives me a big kiss. "That was so cool! Thank you for bringing me here."

He spins me around as I laugh and only puts me down when we're both dizzy. We head back to the cellar door to have one last drink. Over the course of the day, we've drunk three bottles between us, plus a few tastings, so we are well and truly tipsy at this point. A live band is playing music in the far corner of the room, and I don't complain when Henry takes my hand in his for a dance. The grin on my face feels permanent, and I declare that today has been the best date I've ever been on.

We load back into the car with our numerous bottles of wine that we've collected over the day and sit with our legs tangled and fingers intertwined in the back seat. Ten minutes into the drive home, Henry is looking out of the window when suddenly he gasps loudly out of nowhere. Jeremy jumps in his seat and swears.

"Jesus Christ, mate. You alright? Scared me half to death," he says.

"What's wrong?" I ask Henry.

He turns and looks at me and there are tears in his eyes. "I just saw a dead kangaroo on the side of the road."

"Oh…"

His lips turn down and a single tear slips out.

I press my lips together tight to stop the laughter that's bubbling up my throat. The poor man looks absolutely devastated.

"I'm afraid that's quite normal, actually. There's so many of them in the wild, and they just jump straight out in front of you," I tell him, patting his knee.

"I see," he replies solemnly.

"I actually hit one with my car last year and had to have my bonnet replaced. It didn't die, thankfully, it just hopped away as if it hadn't just been hit by a car. I was relieved though, I don't know what I would have done if I had killed one—"

A small sniffle stops me in my tracks and I turn to see Henry is now openly crying.

"Oh my god, Henry, it's okay." I hold him as best as I can, the seatbelt digging into my hip.

"They're just so cute and they're an Australian icon. I can't believe they're left on the side of the road as roadkill."

"Well, some people actually come and collect them to use for dog food on farms…" Jeremy butts in, and the look of horror on both of our faces stops him from saying anything further.

"I'm sorry you had to see that so soon after you got to see a kangaroo for the first time," I say. "How about this? For our fourth date, I'll take you to one of the wildlife sanctuaries we have here so you can see a whole bunch of kangaroos. You can feed them and pat them, maybe even get a selfie. They also have koalas and echidnas… I think you'll love it."

He smiles at me and wipes away his tears. "That sounds like a perfect date. When can we go?"

"Let's check over our calendars when we're both a little more sober, but it will be soon. I promise." I lock my pinkie finger with his and that elicits another smile out of him. He clears his throat and sits up straighter in his seat. "Are you okay?" I ask him, biting my lip.

"I'm good. I wasn't crying, by the way," he says.

"Uh-huh."

"The sun was in my eyes and there was a lot of glare."

"I believe you," I tease.

He huffs out a laugh and we hold hands once more, listening to music and making small talk with Jeremy for the rest of the drive home. Henry rests his hand on my leg, and his fingers gently rub the inside of my thigh. His hand drifts ever so slightly, higher and higher, until his touch starts to feel electric. When I glance in his direction, he's smirking at me. I bite my bottom lip, and he looks down to my mouth and gently rubs his thumb over my cheekbone, and then my mouth, releasing my lip and leaning down to give me a soft, gentle kiss. I sigh into it, and he grips my leg a little harder. I can feel the anticipation building. I'm feeling relaxed, sun-kissed and safe, with this man who moments ago showed more emotion over an animal than any other man I've dated has shown emotion about anything.

Once we arrive back to my house, we unpack the car and thank Jeremy for spending the afternoon with us. I unlock the front door and we dump all of the wine on the dining table. I look at Henry. He looks at me.

One moment, we are standing there staring at each other in complete silence, the next, we are colliding. A mess of tongues and hands, grabbing, touching and kissing like two people starved of affection.

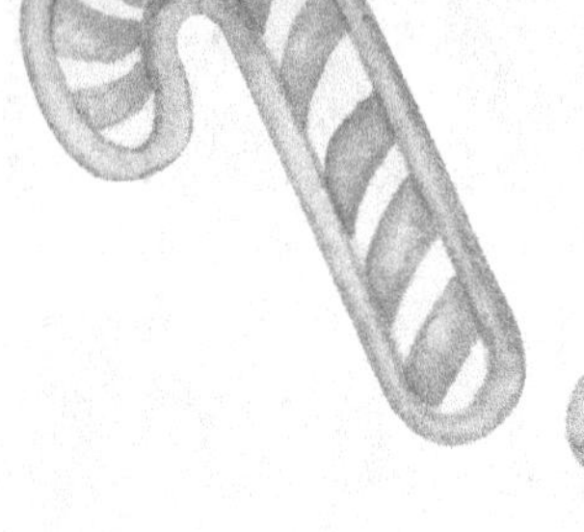

FIVE
Chemistry

"Are you sure about this?" Henry rasps between kisses.

"Positive," I say, kicking off my shoes.

My hands are ripping at his shirt, trying to get it off as fast as possible. His hands are in my hair, and his tongue is in my mouth. He kisses me deeply, causing me to moan into his mouth. I get his shirt free and make quick work of the buttons, throwing it onto the floor and admiring his body in all of its glory. Reaching for his pants, he takes my hand and stops me. I look up into his eyes, and the heat within them sets me alight.

"Are you absolutely sure?" he asks.

"I'm sure. I'm not drunk. I feel safe with you, and I want to do this." I place both hands on his chest and stand up on my tiptoes to kiss him.

"The things I want to do to you…" he whispers in my ear, his hot breath sending shivers down my spine. "I just want to make sure you are completely ready for this." He pauses. "Contraception?"

I tilt my head up and stare at him, grinning wickedly. "I

have an IUD. I am more than ready. I've been horny for you since you first made eye contact with me at that party. Now, take off your pants."

He raises an eyebrow at me.

"Please," I say, fluttering my eyelids.

"Oh, you think you're in charge, do you? Think you can make demands?"

My grin widens. "Maybe."

"We'll see about that."

He picks me up, and I wrap my legs around his waist as he takes me into my bedroom. He throws me onto the bed, and I giggle as I land. I lean back on my elbows and look at him, shirtless and standing at the edge of the bed. He kicks off his shoes one by one, not breaking eye contact.

"Take. Off. Your. Pants," I demand.

"Use. Your. Manners," he replies.

I look up at him through my lashes and pout slightly. "Pretty please, can you take off your pants?"

Henry smirks and grabs a hold of both of my ankles, dragging me to the edge of the bed. I squeal, until he's leaning over me and my breath catches in my throat.

"You want my pants off, sweetheart? You take them off yourself."

Holy hell.

I lick my lips and take my bottom lip between my teeth, as I reach for the button of his shorts and undo it. I slowly pull down the zipper, and then take a hold of the waist band and shove them down. He steps out of them and tilts my chin up with his finger.

"Better?" he asks.

"Almost. These too." I grab a hold of his briefs, his cock already straining, and slowly pull them down, freeing him.

"Much better," I breathe.

I grab a hold of him and he hisses through his teeth, as I lick him from the base all the way to the tip. He takes a fist full of my hair and pulls me back, gentle enough to test my reaction.

"Take your clothes off and then you get to play," he demands.

I smirk, stroking him a few more times before he takes a step back and out of my reach.

"Now, Claudia."

I roll my eyes at him but I do as he says, because I'm desperate. I stand in the middle of the bed and put on a show of taking off my jumpsuit. I undo the zip at my side, slide the shoulder straps down, the fabric tickling my skin and causing goosebumps to erupt along my arms. Ever so slowly, I shimmy the fabric down until it pools at my feet and I'm left standing in my white lace G-string. Henry looks at my body like a man who has been crawling through a desert and has spotted an oasis.

"Like what you see?" I ask.

He says nothing, and he doesn't need to. Instead, he steps closer to the edge of the bed and wraps his hands around my upper thighs. Tracing kisses along the underside of my breasts, I hold my breath in anticipation. His thumbs hook into my underwear and drag them down my legs. I step out of them and then I am bare to him. We are completely naked around each other for the first time, and I've never felt more confident.

"You are exquisite," he hums along my stomach.

"Thank you," I whisper.

"Any more demands?"

I laugh. "Yes, as a matter of fact. I demand that you—"

In an instant, he has me flat on my back on the bed. Climbing on top of me, he pins my arms above my head.

He smirks. "You were saying?"

"Nothing. Absolutely nothing," I pant.

"That's what I thought."

He kisses me, hard, and I melt into him. He releases my arms and my fingers are immediately in his hair, pulling tight. Growling, he starts kissing and nipping at my neck, causing me to squirm.

"So, Claudia, how do you like it?" he asks.

"Oh... I'm not sure."

"Soft and gentle?" he whispers against my skin.

"Hmm..." I whimper as his tongue traces a gentle circle around my nipple.

"Or do you like it a little harder?"

He bites down and I moan, arching my back as a delicious pain spreads through me to my core.

"Both. I want both. I just want you, Henry."

He looks up at me, and in his eyes I see lust, sincerity and... something else. "You have me."

A soft smile creeps up my lips as he continues to kiss his way down my body, until his mouth is inches away from where I so desperately want it to be.

"Henry..."

"Yes?"

"If you don't touch me right now, I'm going to combust."

"Is that another demand?" he teases.

"Yes. Touch me, please."

"Well, since you asked so nicely..."

His tongue is on me in an instant, licking over my clit and sending lightning through my veins. He takes his time building up momentum, figuring out exactly what makes me tick. The pressure, the speed. I don't even have to say anything, he just picks up on my physical cues. Soon, he has built up a rhythm that has me whimpering, my legs clamping around his head.

"As much as I love the idea of being crushed to death between your legs, I want you to be open for me, sweetheart." He forces my legs open and continues to feast on me. Try as I might, I can't close my legs, and it intensifies the feeling building up inside of me tenfold. I can sense my climax nearing, but there's something missing. I need more.

"What do you need, Claudia?" he asks, expertly reading me.

"I need more, I need to feel full," I tell him.

He says nothing, but he slowly inserts a finger inside of me, and then another. My back lifts off the bed as he curls his fingers, finding my G-spot. It's exactly what I need, and it only takes a few pumps of his fingers to send me spiralling over the edge.

"Oh my god. Fuck, yes!" I moan.

My orgasm courses through me, making me feel momentarily weightless. The stubble on Henry's chin scrapes along my inner thigh as he watches me come.

Suddenly, he chuckles against my skin, clearly pleased with his efforts

"Why are you laughing?" I say, breathless.

"I'm not laughing at you. Watching you come undone just now made me so incredibly hot for you."

"Okay. Great!" I give him a thumbs up as I lie on the bed looking at the ceiling, still in my post-orgasm daze.

He laughs again. "We're not done, you know."

"Oh I know. I'm just catching my breath before I ride you into oblivion."

I sit up and pull his face to mine, kissing him hard. His hands are in my hair again, and he pulls slightly. I've never been with a man who gets joy from my pleasure, nor have I been with a man who pulls my hair and throws me around like he has.

I fucking love it.

My hands slide up his torso, skimming over his abs, until I reach his shoulders, and I push him down forcefully so that he's lying on his back. I swing my leg over his hips and straddle him, smirking.

"My turn," I tell him, and the man simply grins and puts his hands behind his head like he's about to have a nap in the sun.

I lean forward and gently put my lips to his, and as I slowly sit back up, I scrape my nails down his chest and to his abdomen, leaving a line of pink scratches in their wake. He inhales sharply, his stomach clenches and his cock twitches beneath me. I smile at him devilishly.

"We are going to have fun, I think. Don't you?" I ask sweetly, as I slide over his length. I'm still slick from my orgasm, and he rolls his eyes and takes in a deep breath with the sensation.

"Fuck, Claudia, you're so fucking wet for me. Yes, I think we are going to have a lot of fun together. And…" He grits his teeth.

"And?"

"And, I hope, for so much more than just *fun*. You are more than just a good time, Claudia. I want everything. I want to experience all of you."

I slow my momentum, taking in the sight of this man beneath me. A warm feeling spreads over me, and my heart starts to pound in my chest.

"You want more?" I whisper.

"Yes," he breathes. "As much as you're willing to give me."

I lean down so I'm lying on top of him and kiss him again; except this time it's a kiss filled with something *more*.

"I want more too," I say against his lips.

"Be mine." He doesn't say it as a question, but more of a command.

I take a moment to really look at him. This man who came into my life so unexpectedly, who still poses a risk to my heart with his lack of permanent residency, but who has me completely under his spell. I want him. I want to be his.

"I'm yours."

We press our foreheads together, and I take in this moment. Skin to skin, with nothing between us. Breathing in each other's air, we stay still and silent for a beat.

I sit up and grin. "Now that's been decided, are you ready for me?"

He gives me a deadpan look and bucks his hips, causing me to wobble and nearly fall to the side.

"I know you can feel how hard I am beneath you. You know how ready I am."

I slide myself onto him again, aligning myself and lifting my hips so he's gently pressed against my entrance.

"Are you sure?" I ask as I sink down ever so slowly, the tip of him entering me.

"I'm. Sure," he says between laboured breaths, taking a hold of my hips.

"Are you really sure? Because—"

He squeezes his hands tight around my hips and pushes into me. I gasp at the sudden fullness, clenching around him as I get used to the sensation of him being inside me so deep.

"Fuck!" he shouts. "You feel so fucking good."

"Henry," I moan, my teeth sinking into my bottom lip.

"Ride me, sweetheart. Ride me like you're mine."

I start to rock back and forth, finding a rhythm that hits just right. He fills me so deliciously, and soon his hips are lifting in sync with me, hitting me deep and exactly where I need him to be.

"Oh god, Henry. I didn't think it could feel this good," I whimper.

"You are a goddess," he groans.

His fingers are digging into my hips so hard now, I'm sure they're going to leave marks. Changing rhythms, I start to bounce up and down on his cock, our skin slapping together with every movement. Sweat starts to bead down my spine, and my thighs are burning, but I can't stop. I won't stop. Because the pleasure shooting through my body is unparalleled. He thrusts his hips up into me, matching my pace and finding pleasure in places I didn't even know possible.

The familiar feelings of an orgasm start to claw their way up, beginning in my toes and making me cry out in pure bliss. This is a different feeling, familiar yet… not. I've never had an orgasm from penetration before, but something is happening, and it feels so fucking good.

"I can feel you, Claudia. I can feel you clenching around my cock," he pants, squeezing my hips tighter and slamming up into me even harder.

I try to say something, but all that comes out are sounds that can only be classified as animalistic.

"I'm going to make you come, sweetheart. You're going to come on my cock, and then I'm going to come. The only question is where?" he says, his voice straining.

I continue bouncing as my climax gets nearer and nearer. My face feels hot, my skin too tight, the blood rushing to my head and causing stars to appear in my vision.

"Where do you want me to come, Claudia? Tell me."

I moan. "Henry…"

"Tell me."

"Fill me up, Henry. I want all of you."

"Fuck. *Fuck!*" he rasps.

I cry out, my orgasm washing over me in wave after destructive wave. My toes curl, and I grip onto his chest, digging my nails in as I ride the crest. I can feel myself tightening around him, and seconds later, he spills himself into me, thrusting up slowly and yelling my name.

We ease off, and I lay myself on top of him, feeling his cock twitch inside of me. We both lay panting for a moment, catching our breaths and coming down from what I am declaring as the best sexual experience I've had in a long, long time.

I lift my head and look at him. He tucks the loose tendrils of my hair behind my ear, and we both laugh. We give each other a high-five, because that was worth celebrating.

"Holy shit," I breathe.

"Holy shit, indeed."

Taking me with him, Henry rolls over to his side and slowly pulls out of me. He kisses me on the tip of my nose before getting up and retrieving a wet wash cloth from my bathroom, where he then proceeds to clean me up. He throws the cloth into the washing basket and slides back into the bed next to me, pulling me in for a cuddle.

We lie in comfortable silence for a beat. My eyes begin to grow heavy with exhaustion.

"That was incredible," I whisper to him.

"It was. I knew we had chemistry… but wow. Not bad eh?"

"Not bad at all." I giggle, and we lie in silence once more.

I close my eyes and listen to the sound of him breathing. My cheek rests upon his chest, and I can feel his heartbeat pounding against my skin.

"So. It's official," he says.

"Yes, it is. Any regrets?"

"Absolutely none. I have you all to myself now." He pauses. "You were such an unexpected surprise."

"Is that a good thing?" I laugh nervously.

"Yes. I didn't expect to meet someone so soon, but you have enchanted me. I'm so glad I jumped into that pool."

Butterflies swarm in my belly and suddenly I'm feeling hot again.

"I'm glad I fell into the pool. I definitely wasn't expecting you. You're… pretty great," I tell him.

"Thank you."

"But I'm still scared," I admit.

"I know." He kisses my forehead. "I know that the future is uncertain. And I know that there may be some things to consider later down the track. But right now, right here with you? I'm so fucking happy."

"I am too."

At some point, Henry gets up to turn off the bedroom light and fill up my drink bottle, knowing I will need to hydrate in the middle of the night. He climbs back into bed and curls himself around me.

I feel safe and warm, and well on my way to falling in love with this man. I just hope that my heart, mind and body allow me, and he doesn't hurt me in the process.

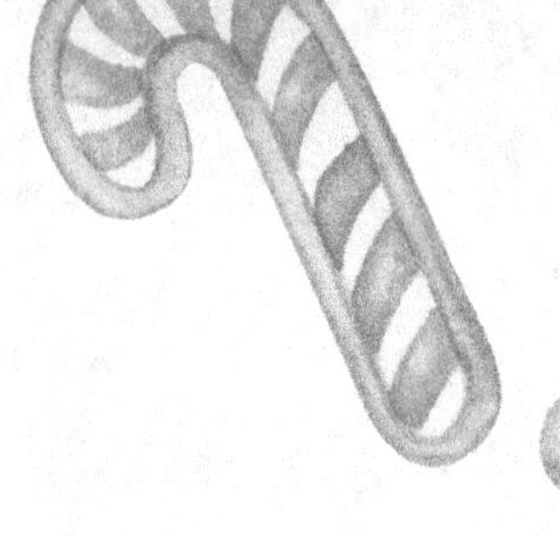

SIX
Easter
2024

"He said yes!" I yell from my kitchen.

"Hell yeah. About damn time," replies Frankie.

"Wait, who said yes? To what?" asks Nath.

"Henry's coming camping with us," I say, coming over to the dining table with dip and crackers.

I've been waiting to see if he can get the Easter weekend off to come camping with us at Deep Creek. It's one of our annual camping trips. Oliver is coming with us too; he and Frankie are seemingly on steady ground at the moment. So this year it looks like it will be the five of us, instead of our usual three.

"Awesome. Guess I really will be the third wheel. Or fifth wheel." Nath pouts.

"You're our spare tyre," I tell him, kissing him on the top of his head and taking the seat next to him.

"You never know, Nath, the group who camped next to us last year might be there again. I'm sure you'll find someone to keep you company," Frank teases.

"Oh I'm not worried. I think it's going to be great," he says, digging into the hummus.

"Me too," I say. "I can't wait to see how Henry handles camping in the Australian bush. He saw a garden spider the other day and I've never seen a grown man jump so high. I think he might faint when he sees a huntsman for the first time."

"As long as there's no snakes again, I'm happy." Nath shudders.

A snake slithered through our campsite last year, and Nath screeched like a banshee so loud it woke up the kids at the campsite three sites down. The parents were furious and stormed over to us, ripping us a new one for disturbing their peace. It was hilarious.

"I'm hoping for some more kangaroos. I need him to see another live one to heal him from the trauma of seeing the roadkill," I tell them. I did take him to the wildlife sanctuary as promised, and he's now even more obsessed with kangaroos.

Frankie smiles. "I'm so glad he's coming, Claud. You seem so happy."

"I am happy. He's… incredible. I don't want to push it though. He's still not sure how long he's going to stay here. Is entering into a rclationship with a temporary citizen really a good idea?" I worry my bottom lip.

"It's been almost five months since you guys met. He's obsessed with you and everyone can see it. I think you're overthinking things. He makes you happy, and what will be will be," she says, as if it's no big deal.

"You're probably right. I just worry, you know? After Peter, I don't want to waste any more time."

"I know, babe. But from what you've said about Henry, he's not the sort of guy to do that. Probably because he's Canadian, and they're supposedly the nicest people in the world." She winks, and I chuckle.

"True. He is very, very nice."

"And tall. And hot," Nath chimes in.

"Yeah." I grin, remembering our first night after our wine tour. Now *that* was hot.

Nath sees the look on my face, noticeably my horny eyes, and makes a declaration.

"New rule for camping. If the tent's rocking, don't come knocking."

We all laugh.

Henry and I have hardly had any time apart since we decided we were exclusive. We see each other every week. I've taken him to some of my favourite spots in the city, we went to a comedy show at the Fringe Festival, and we've gone snorkelling at Port Noarlunga. He stays at my house most weekends, and I'm so accustomed to him sleeping next to me now that I struggle to fall asleep if he's not there.

Last weekend, we were lying in bed, our bodies still warm from the mind-blowing sex we'd just had, music playing softly in the background as we stared into each other's eyes. Out of nowhere, I felt this sudden, overwhelming urge to cry. A single tear slipped out, and Henry gently brushed it away with a kiss. I was flooded with so many feelings for this man that I almost told him I loved him right then and there. But I didn't have to. He tucked a strand of hair behind my ear and simply whispered, "*I know.*"

***

We arrive at our campsite just before the sun starts to set, which thankfully means we can set up in the daylight, unlike last year. We pitch our tent with ease, setting up the rest of the site and getting started on cooking dinner, before settling down with a game of Phase 10. The entire campground is full, some with families and caravans, there's a boy's trip two spots down from us with six swags all lined up together, and then there's other groups like us. Nath has already done some scouting and has teed up drinks with our neighbours for tomorrow night. Our first night is a quiet one, and we're all exhausted and in bed by 10pm. I fall asleep in Henry's arms.

The smell of bacon and eggs cooking on the BBQ the next morning revives me as we start our first full day. Nath is cooking for us, and I'm on coffee duty. No matter where I am, coffee is a must for me first thing in the morning. I can't stand instant coffee, so I purchased a plunger and ground coffee beans so I can actually have something decent, even when camping. I pour us each a cup, except Henry, who I have discovered can't stand coffee and is strictly a tea drinker. Sitting at the table, we plan our day over breakfast. The weather is looking perfect, and there's a hike I really want to take Henry on. It leads to a gorgeous water hole, and it's still just warm enough that we can probably swim in it.

"If we get ready straight after breakfast, we should get to the water hole by lunchtime," Frankie says. "We can eat, swim, and then by the time we get back it'll be time for drinks and shenanigans."

"Sounds good to me. Henry, are you ready for your first Australian hike?" I ask.

"Ready as I'll ever be," he says.

Changing into our activewear, we pack our bikinis and a picnic lunch and head out onto the track. It takes us about an hour and a half to get there. It's a relatively easy hike, but as it is Henry's first true Australian bush experience, we take our time and let him take it all in. We spot a few koalas napping in the gum trees, and a monitor lizard lazily cuts across the track ahead of us – Nath thinks it's a snake at first and nearly falls on his ass to get away from it. The weather is perfect, the sun is shining brightly, but the shade of the trees keeps the harshness of it at bay.

"Do you think the waterfall will be flowing?" I ask, slightly out of breath as we descend the steep hill.

"Maybe, the huge downpour we had last week may have been enough to get it going," Nath says.

"I hope it is. I'm sweating up a storm back here," Frankie whines. She's always the first to suggest a hike, and always the first to complain.

"We're almost there. I remember this part from the last time I did this," I tell her.

After ten more minutes of stumbling our way down the mountain, we hear the rushing sound of water falling over rock. We come around the bend, and the water hole comes into view. The waterfall is in fact flowing steadily, and the water looks cool and fresh, and we all sigh in relief. I'm surprised to find no one else is here either.

"Oh this is perfect," Frankie says. Henry appears to be in complete awe, taking in his surroundings.

This hike is one of my favourites for a reason, and Mother Nature really is turning it on for us today. Layers of limestone and granite surround the waterhole, creating a small but enticing pool of water just deep enough to swim in. The gumtrees here are old and stand tall overhead, giving us the perfect amount of shade. Native flora is dotted among the boughs of the trees, and it's so calm and peaceful. We drop our bags on a large flat rock and duck behind a few trees to get dressed into our bathers.

Nath is the first one in the water, charging his way in and promptly destroying the tranquillity with his shouts of protest once the cold water hits his nether regions. Frankie and Oliver settle themselves on a rock to soak up the sun, and I take Henry's hand.

"Are you ready?" I ask.

"There isn't anything in that water that could kill me, right?" he asks nervously, and I laugh.

"No. There's no crocodiles or leeches. Snakes can swim, but Nath is making enough noise that I don't imagine we will come across one. You're safe."

We walk hand in hand around the edge of the water. As we do, I point out local plants and tell him the history of the area. The water gushing over the edge of the cliff isn't too loud, creating a soft sort of ambience to the otherwise quiet and serene space. Finding an edge that doesn't look too slippery, we tentatively step into the water, inhaling sharply as we find it to actually be quite fucking cold indeed.

"I told you!" Nath shouts at us.

"Think of it like a cold plunge," Henry says.

"I hate cold plunges," I whine.

"Let's go under at least once, and then we can lie out on the rocks and soak up the sun again," he suggests.

"Okay. Good plan."

"One... two... three."

We both sink down into the icy water and swear, loudly, as goosebumps erupt all over my skin. My teeth start to clatter immediately, but I swim around to try and warm myself up a bit. After a few minutes, my body adjusts to the cool temperature and it actually feels sort of pleasant. It has washed away the sweat from the hike down the mountain, and my muscles have started relaxing a little. Henry swims up to me, and I instinctively wrap my legs around his thighs and my arms around his neck, kissing him softly.

"Hi," I breathe.

"Hi," he replies, a cheeky glint in his eye.

"Gross!" Nath yells at us, splashing in our direction as he starts to swim to the other side of the waterhole.

I squeal and duck out of the spray of the water, and the top half of my body comes up out of the water. Henry's eyes immediately fall to my chest, where my nipples are peaked from the cold water and poking through my bikini.

Looking back up into my eyes, his gaze is piercing and I know the look that crosses over his face. Desire and hunger. I squeeze my legs tighter around his waist, closing the distance between us, and I feel him hardening beneath me, despite the temperature of the water.

"How are you able to get it up right now? It's freezing!" I giggle.

"Because," he leans in, lips brushing over the shell of my ear, "you are wrapped around me, our bodies separated by scraps of fabric, your hard nipples are scraping across my chest." I shiver. "And also, because you are so fucking beautiful that I struggle to keep myself contained when I am around you."

He pulls me tighter to him and kisses me so deeply it makes my head spin. I meet his energy and slide my tongue into his mouth, slowly grinding myself against his lap. His hands roam across my bare back, and I grip his hair, pulling slightly. He groans and squeezes my arse as I continue to grind. He pulls away, slightly breathless.

"You keep doing that and any restraint I do have will disintegrate," he growls.

"Sorry." I smile devilishly, grinding on him again.

"Sure you are."

"Can you two fucking not?" Frankie yells. "I came here to immerse myself in nature, not watch you fuck in a water hole."

We both chuckle as we break apart slightly, though I keep my legs wrapped around Henry's waist. He grips onto my hips and doesn't let go, resting his forehead on mine and taking a breath.

"This is one of my favourite places to go," I tell him.

"I can see why. It's gorgeous. Not too loud but calming."

"I find the sound of rushing water soothing. It sort of forces my brain to quieten. Does that make sense?"

"It does. It's like it shuts out all of the other noise."

We bask in the sounds of the bush around us for a moment, listening to the rush of water, the rustling of leaves and a magpies song creating its own unique sense of peace.

I hear Henry take in a deep breath. "I want to ask you something. It probably seems a little redundant now, and we've already had a similar conversation but, um, I still want to ask it," he says shyly.

"Okay…"

"I know we have already said that we are exclusive, and I also feel like I'm too old to ask this question, now that I think about it, but here it goes. Claudia, will you be my girlfriend?"

I smile, and then I giggle. "You want me to be your girlfriend?" I ask.

"I do. I really, really do. I know it sounds silly but I just wanted to hear the words. We've been together for nearly five months now and I just feel so deeply for you—"

"Okay," I tell him.

"Okay?"

"Yeah. I'll be your girlfriend."

We both smile from ear to ear. Despite the fact that I had already started referring to Henry as my boyfriend, something about him wanting to ask me outright makes my heart swell. It's reassuring, in a way.

Eventually, once my toes start to feel a bit numb, we climb out of the water and lie ourselves down on the rocks to soak up the sun and dry off. We eat our picnic lunch and then, when we're full, we start to slowly make our way back up the mountain. By the time we reach the top, we are all ready for a drink, and for the party to start.

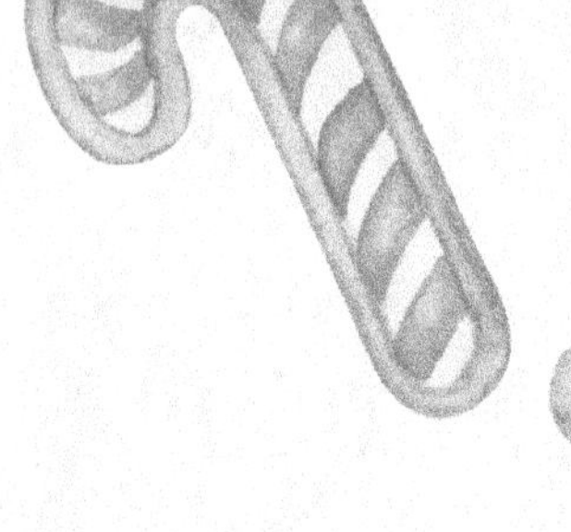

SEVEN
Declarations

"Can I open my eyes yet?" Henry asks, the sound of bark and gum leaves crunching underfoot as I drag him through the bush to a secret location.

"Almost… Okay. Now you can open your eyes."

Blinking as he adjusts to his surroundings, Henry gasps at the sight before him.

"I wanted to create a special night just for us, to show you the magic of camping in the Australian bush. Do you like it?"

"It's… wonderful."

I've created our own little corner of the campgrounds, far enough away from the other campers that they can't see us but we can still faintly hear them. I dragged a swag mattress over for us to sit on, and a small amount of wood for us to create our own mini camp fire. The fire restrictions lifted a week before Easter, but I bought a small fire drum to use, just to be safe.

"I've got some marshmallows and some wine. I figured we could light a small fire and just cuddle up and have some quiet time by ourselves, just for a little while."

"That sounds perfect."

We settle down onto the swag, and I reach into the bag I'd brought over to retrieve the marshmallows. I instruct Henry to go and find the absolute best marshmallow roasting sticks he can find, as I start getting the fire ready. I have to send him away three times before he finally comes back with the perfect sticks. He pours us each a mug of wine (no wine glasses when camping, too risky) and settles back while I try and stoke the flames. I can feel him staring at me as I go through the motions of stacking the kindling and smaller branches, lighting the fire starters and feeding the flames ever so slowly, as to not put them out before they truly take. He takes in a deep breath and then leans back on his elbows, his head tilting up to the sky.

"Oh. My. God," he breathes.

I look at him and then tilt my head back to see what has him so entranced. I break into a smile, because the skies are so clear tonight, and the moon shines brightly. Though it does not at all compare to the constellation twinkling high above us. The Milky Way is scattered across the night sky, creating a sea of glitter in the otherwise pure darkness.

"Wow. We can see the stars at home but this, this is something else," he says, astonished.

"Nothing beats stargazing, especially when camping. Any time I feel stressed, I just take myself out of the city and find somewhere to sleep under the stars. They have a way of making me feel so small and insignificant, but in some weird sense it helps me feel grounded and reminds me that although I am but a small part within a large moving world, I do matter." I stare hard into the smattering sea of soft yellows and blues and oranges. I could stare at the stars all night. We sit in silence for a moment, soaking it all in.

"Have a look and see if you can find the Southern Cross," I tell him.

I continue to feed the fire as he searches the sky, pointing out clusters of stars that don't even closely resemble the cross. I spotted it immediately, almost like I'd been trained my whole life to be able to find it easily. I place a small log onto the fire, and lean closer to Henry. Pointing up into the sky, I show him where to find the constellation.

"The Southern Cross is right… there. See? The four bright stars and then the fifth, more subtle star." I make a cross pattern in the sky, in front of his eye line.

"I can see it now. That's so cool. And what's that one?" he asks, pointing to another bright spot.

I squint. And then laugh. "That's a plane."

"Oh."

"That one over there is Mars. And that one there is the Saucepan."

"The Saucepan? I've never heard of that one."

"Really?" I furrow my brow. "I thought it was one of the more popular ones."

"Hmm." He looks again at where I'm pointing. "Wait, I'm pretty sure that's Orion's Belt." He gets out his phone to look it up, and laughs. "Yep. It's Orion's Belt. Though according to the internet, Australian's call it the Saucepan."

"Well then. You learn something new every day. I think Saucepan is a better name for it though."

"I agree. Now, marshmallows?"

Our small fire is burning hot enough that we are able to skewer our marshmallows and toast them over the flames. I like mine to be almost charcoal on the outside before I eat it, so I allow it to catch alight and smoulder for a few seconds before blowing it out. Peeling it slowly off the stick, I make sure it isn't too hot before parting my lips and shoving the whole thing in. The crisp, burnt outside contrasts with the sweet and gooey inside, and I moan in delight at the sweetness exploding in my mouth. My fingers are sticky with pink residue, and Henry takes my hand. He looks me in the eye as he sucks the sugary goodness off of one finger, and then the next. Need pulses through me, and heat flushes my cheeks, though not from the fire.

"My sweet," he whispers, and a slight moan escapes me.

He grins, and pops his own marshmallow in his mouth, quickly swallowing before pulling me into his lap. We kiss, mouths sticky and sugary, and my heart starts racing. It's like this every time he touches me. My body craves him constantly and then when he touches me, I go into overdrive.

"Every day I'm so glad I met you. I hope you know that, Claudia."

"I do," I say shyly, unsure of how to take the compliment.

He tucks some of my loose hair behind my ear and places his palm against my cheek. I lean into his touch, closing my eyes and savouring his closeness.

"You fell into my life, quite literally. I came to this country looking for adventure, and to try something new. Never in my wildest dreams did I think I would meet someone. Let alone meet you…" He pauses, tilting my face towards his and looking into my eyes. I see the bob of his Adam's apple as he swallows hard. "Never did I ever imagine that I would fall in love."

I inhale sharply. "What?" I whisper.

"I love you, Claudia. I think I fell for you the moment you gawked at me at that party." He smiles softly. His thumb traces over my bottom lip, which has dropped open in surprise at his declaration.

"Henry…"

"You don't have to say it back," he tells me. "Some might say it's too early to make declarations of love, but I just know. And I didn't want to hold back." He kisses me gently, his palm caressing the side of my cheek. We rest our foreheads together, and I focus on the sound of his breathing to calm my racing heart.

"I love you too," I say, barely audible over the crackling of the flames.

Henry's eyes shoot up and lock onto mine, the glacial blue of his irises sparkle in the fire light.

"You do?" he asks.

"I do. It just feels… right. I love you, Henry."

Henry's smile brightens up the entire space as he pulls me in tight. We kiss and laugh and bask in the joy that is a confession of love.

Our kisses soon turn heated, his tongue sliding over mine, my teeth nipping at his bottom lip. Henry takes off his shirt and slowly takes off mine. I'm naked underneath, and I shiver, despite the flames at my back. There's no one around, and I made sure we weren't visible from any campsites when I set up our little spot. And so, beneath the glittering Milky Way and by the light of the campfire, Henry and I make love under the stars. Our bodies move together as one, our breaths synchronising, our climaxes bringing us together in the most beautiful and harmonious way. And as I lie there in his arms, naked and content, I allow myself the chance to dream of a happily ever after.

PART TWO

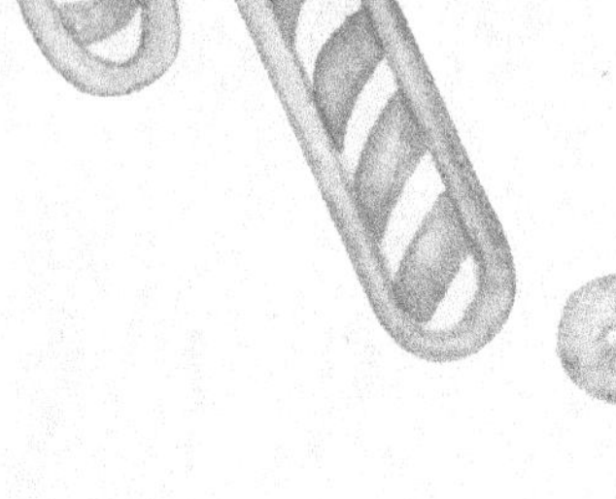

EIGHT
December 1st
2024

We walk into the bar, a place called Jimmies that apparently makes killer cocktails, and find Gabi and Eric sitting in the beer garden, already with a drink in hand.

"Hey, big sis!" Gabi says, standing to give me a hug. She squeezes me so tight she almost crushes my boobs and I have to shove her off me.

"Ouch, Gab. Hi, what's with the crushing?" I ask, stepping aside to give Henry room to hug her as well.

"I missed you, that's all." She beams.

"It hasn't been that long," I say, squinting my eyes in suspicion. She's never this affectionate, verbally or physically.

Eric clears his throat and leans in to give me a hug. "Hey, Claud. Hope you're doing alright."

"I'm really good, ready for a drink though. Are you guys all good? We'll get one and then meet you at the table."

"Yep, we're good," says Gabi, who promptly rushes to sit back down.

"Weird," I mutter to Henry.

"What's weird?"

"Gabi. She's never affectionate. Something must be wrong."

"Oh right. Well let's get our drinks so we can figure it out."

We go up to the bar and order two cocktails from the bartender, who after chatting with, we find out is also the owner. He recommended his signature cocktail, named after his wife Ella, and we take them over to the table. Gabi is bouncing in her seat, and there is definitely something wrong. She is oozing nervous energy.

"Alright spit it out," I say. "What's wrong? You're all jumpy."

"Nothing's wrong!" she says, and I give her my deadpan look that she absolutely despises. "I'm serious. Nothing's wrong. I got you something." She slides over a small bag.

"It's not Christmas yet."

"I know, but I wanted to give this to you early because I can't help myself." She clasps her hands together in front of her face.

I open the bag and pull out the tissue paper. Inside is a small box, and the second I open it and see what's inside, I burst into tears.

"Really?!" I sob.

"Really!" Gabi crics.

Henry's head swivels between the two of us, confused. Even Eric is tearing up.

"What? What's happening?" Henry asks.

I pass him the box, inside sits a delicate gold bracelet with a single ruby charm, next to the word *Aunty*.

"You're pregnant!" I yell.

She nods enthusiastically, too overwhelmed to respond.

We stand at the same time, both a blubbering mess. I hug her so tightly and then pull back because I don't want to crush my new niece or nephew.

"How far along? When are you due? Oh my god, I'm going to be an aunty!" I squeal.

"I'm due in July. I'm about seven or eight weeks along."

"But I saw you a month ago!"

"We didn't know yet, we literally found out the next day," Eric chimed in. I've never seen him look so happy.

"Congrats, guys. This is the best news in the whole world. I'm so happy for you." I pull her in for a hug again, and gesture for Eric and Henry to join us for a group hug. We all get one big squeeze in before pulling away and sitting back down again.

"You're the only one who knows," Gabi says. "I plan on announcing it at Christmas lunch."

"Oh perfect, get it all done in one go," I say, lifting my glass.

"I want you to be there when I do."

I pause with my drink halfway to my lips and frown. "I'm supposed to be with Dad for Christmas this year," I tell her.

"I know. I've already said that Eric and I will be doing Christmas Eve dinner with him this year, and he's happy with that, said he will take us to Lobethal like we did when we were kids. You could join us? We'll be telling him and his side of the family before we tell Mum's side."

The all too familiar feeling of guilt begins to swirl in my gut. The pressure to please everyone and not let anyone down, rises to the surface.

"I don't know, Gabi. Two years of skipping Christmas with Dad, you know how I feel about that." Henry places a hand on my knee and gives it a gentle squeeze. I've already given him the spiel.

"I know. I know I'm asking for a lot, but I really want you to be there. You know what Mum's side is like. I need you there."

Well, if my little sister needs me… how the hell do I say no to that? I sigh in resignation, and she already knows I'm going to say yes.

"Fine…"

"Thank you, thank you, thank you!" She beams.

"You owe me one."

"I know. This means so much to me, Claud. I love you forever."

"I love you forever and a day." I smile. It's something we've said to each other ever since our parents divorced.

Henry helps to clasp my new bracelet onto my wrist, sending shivers across my skin when his hand lingers. The boys start talking about sport or something, and Gabi and I go into full baby mode.

"You're not mad at me?" she asks hesitantly.

"Why would I be mad at you?" I respond, confused.

"Because I know this is something you've wanted for a long time, and here I am, the baby sister, married and pregnant."

My heart sinks.

"Oh my god, no. I'm not mad at you, not one little bit. Life didn't go how I planned it to, and that's okay. I'm okay with it. I can't spend my life living in comparison with others, so don't you worry about that. Okay?"

She smiles at me and takes my hand. "Okay. I guess you do have this one keeping you company now. Who knows, there might be a whole lot of this in your near future," she says as she dramatically rubs her belly.

I laugh, and look across nervously to Henry, who is also laughing with genuine glee. I think it's high time I start trusting that this man isn't going to screw me around, and that he does genuinely want the same things that I do. I relax and lean in for a kiss. He smiles down at me, and in that moment I feel really, truly, content.

***

It's almost dinner by the time we get back to my house. Henry is staying the night and has declared he's in charge of cooking, which I will never say no to.

"I'm really excited for you, sweetheart. You're going to be the best aunt."

"Thanks. I can't wait."

It's true. I'm so excited to be an aunty, and I wasn't lying to

Gabi when I said I wasn't mad at her. There is, unfortunately, that little niggling voice in my head that's telling me that this should have been me making an announcement. I'm the one they all expected to get married and have babies first. And maybe it's because of that external pressure, but there is a feeling of failure beginning to creep in.

"You okay?" Henry asks, noticing the shift in my body language.

"Yeah, I'm fine. I am excited. I just…"

"You just wish it was you?" he says, saying the words I'm yet to say out loud.

I nod, ashamed.

"That's a totally normal feeling. I'm sure every older sister who has ever been in your situation has felt that way. It doesn't make you a bad person, or any less happy for Gabi. It just makes you human." He pulls me into a hug, wiping away the traitorous tear that escaped down my cheek.

"When did you become so wise?" I sniff.

"I was born this way." He shrugs, and I laugh.

"You're right though," I tell him. "I'm probably not the only one who's felt this way. I'm just going to process my feelings so I can enter into this era of my life fully supportive and enthusiastic."

"Good plan. After all, comparison is the thief of joy. Your time will come, don't you worry about that."

He kisses the tip of my nose and sends me off to have a shower as he prepares dinner, and with those words, I let myself feel what I'm feeling. Happy, disappointed, jealous, glad, all normal feelings for a situation like this. I let it all wash over me, until I settle on overwhelming joy for my baby sister.

Now I just have to get through another family Christmas. It'll be fine. I have a man by my side this year. What could go wrong?

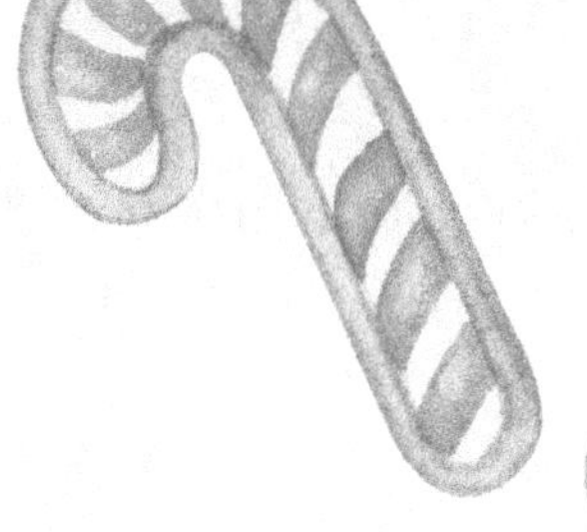

NINE
Christmas Eve
2024

"It's so hot," Henry whines.

"Yes. Welcome to an Australian Christmas!" I tell him.

"You were here last summer," Gabi chimes in.

"Yeah, but I forgot how disgusting it is. Plus this just feels weird, driving to see Christmas lights when it's 32 degrees at 9pm."

"I will admit, it is ridiculously hot tonight, and it seems it isn't going to cool down much tomorrow either," I say.

"At least we'll have the pool, right?" Henry asks, hopeful.

"Sure will."

"Are you excited about your first Australian Christmas, Henry?" Dad asks.

"I am. I love Christmas, and I can't wait to see how different it is here."

My dad's side of the family love a traditional hot Christmas dinner, so we've already gorged ourselves on roast turkey and vegetables, smothered in gravy with mounds of pork crackling. We sat around the table, air conditioning on full speed, telling bad jokes and filling Henry in on the lore of our family. Not quite the traditional Australian Christmas – that will come tomorrow – but it was so wholesome to see him getting along with my family.

Gabi announced her pregnancy at dinner, and everyone was overwhelmed with joy. Eventually, my grandma served up Christmas pudding, which I hate, so I had a bowl of custard for dessert instead. Now, we've said goodbye to the extended family and are going on a drive to show Henry the famous Lobethal Christmas Lights. We've stuffed ourselves into Dad's seven-seater, and he's playing tour guide.

"So you love Christmas, and you've ended up with Miss Grinch back there. How's that going so far?" Dad jokes.

Everyone laughs and I chuckle awkwardly, keeping the hurtful sting hidden beneath a fake smile. Henry reaches across the seat and takes my hand. They should all know by now exactly why I hate Christmas. I'm grateful Dad's side of the family were happy to do a Christmas Eve dinner with us at the last minute, but there were still a few comments made about making sure next year we spend Christmas Day together *for once*.

"It's going great, actually," Henry starts. "She's made my first Christmas here feel very special. I know she has her own feelings about it, but she doesn't let that impact on anyone else's experience because she wants the best day for everyone. You have quite the selfless daughter here, Arthur."

Dad smiles and looks at me in the rear-view mirror. "That sounds about right. My Claudia, always making sure everyone is happy and enjoying themselves."

I smile back at him, somewhat melancholy. That's me: selfless, always putting other people first, making sure I please everyone.

Henry squeezes my hand and leans in to whisper in my ear, "It's about time someone starts taking care of you, sweetheart. I hope you'll let me."

He places a kiss atop my shoulder and I smile, properly this time. Tears prick the back of my eyes and kiss him on the cheek.

"I'll try," I whisper back.

We get to Lobethal and by some miracle, we find somewhere to park our car. Spotting an ice cream van, we decide that we haven't quite had enough to eat tonight and a second dessert is needed. Hand in hand, Henry and I walk with my family to view the spectacular displays of Christmas lights and music. The intricate detail that goes into preparing for this festival is awe inspiring. It's the first time I've been here since I was a teenager, and it reminds me of why I used to love Christmas. The look of joy and wonder on the kids' faces makes me miss the innocence of childhood.

This used to be my favourite time of year. I remember vividly walking around here with my mum and dad, holding their hands and being swung high in the air, making me laugh so much that tears would roll down my cheeks. When my parents divorced, Mum stopped coming but Dad kept up the Christmas light tradition. Gabi was a few years younger than me and he still wanted to make sure she never lost the spirit of Christmas, despite mine having disappeared. I ache to feel that sort of joy again.

"You okay?" Henry asks.

"Yeah. Just reminiscing." I smile sadly.

"I'm glad we're here. Thank you for bringing me." He kisses me softly.

"I'm glad we came. It's been a long time. I tripped and fell on that curb over there when I was eight." I point to a house decorated with lit up Christmas sweets. "The family who lived there heard me crying and gave me a chocolate cookie, one they were going to leave out for Santa." I smile fondly at the memory.

"A lot of memories here then?" he asks.

"So many. It was our family tradition."

"We could start our own traditions."

I look up at him. "Really?"

"Yeah. I want to bring back the joy of Christmas. I want to erase the bad memories and replace them with new ones."

"I'd love that."

We walk around some more and finish our ice creams, mine almost melted into a puddle by the time I finish it.

"The cold hurts my teeth, I have to eat it slow!" I tell Henry, who just stands there laughing at me as I constantly have to lick the dripping ice cream from the cone.

I clean myself up with a napkin and find my dad, who is standing and inspecting the structural engineering of a sleigh pulled by nine robotic reindeer.

"I'm glad we did this," he says, putting an arm around my shoulder. "It reminds me of when you were younger. You loved this place so much."

"I know. A lot has changed since then."

"It sure has." He turns to look at Henry, who is standing and chatting with Gabi and Eric. "I think you've picked a good one with him. Much better than that other loser."

I laugh. "Yeah, infinitely better than the other loser. There's just one problem."

"He's blonde?"

I smack him on the arm.

"Sorry! Sorry. I just always thought you had a thing for dark and brooding. Henry is more of a golden retriever. What's the problem?"

"Yes, well it appears my taste has changed. The big obvious problem. He's from Canada, and he's only here temporarily. He has a life back in Almonte, responsibilities that he can't run away from forever. Meaning this…" I gesture around to every-thing. "… will come to an end soon enough."

"You don't know that for sure though," Dad says.

I turn and look back at Henry again. He catches me looking and smiles that big megawatt smile I love so much. I grin back.

"No, I don't. But in my experience, everything is temporary."

"Well, maybe you should make a Christmas wish just like you used to. Let a little bit of magic in your life again, Claudia. You never know what might happen."

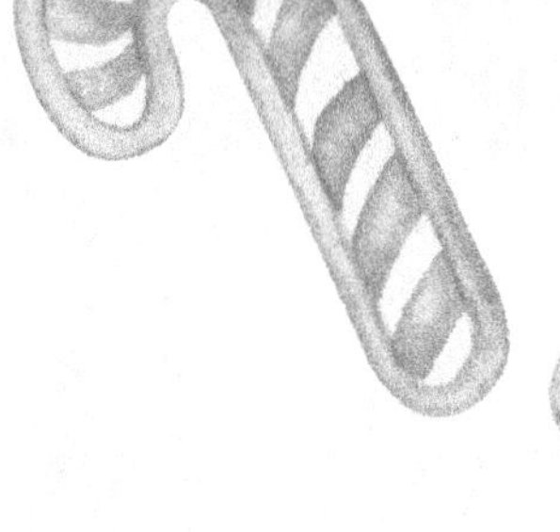

TEN
Christmas Day
2024

"I can't do it."

"Yes, you can."

"Nope, nope, nope!"

I shake my head and yank off the dress I'm wearing, turning to my wardrobe to rummage for another outfit.

It's Christmas morning. Henry and I woke up together and he set up a beautiful breakfast, complete with his signature chocolate croissants and freshly brewed coffee. We exchanged gifts. I bought him tickets for a helicopter flight over the Barossa Valley, complete with a self-guided mystery wine tour, seeing as we loved the last one so much. He got me a beautiful gold necklace with both of our initials as charms, as well as a basket of all of my favourite snacks and self-care products. I may have cried a little. We're now getting ready to go to Aunty Kathy's house, and I'm trying to pick out my outfit.

"What was wrong with that dress?" Henry asks, sitting on the edge of the bed refolding all of the outfits I've tried on and discarded.

"It was too loose and flowy."

"And that's bad because…"

"Because if it's too loose and flowy they will think I'm trying to hide a baby bump," I tell him.

"Right. And the yellow dress?" He holds up the dress I had on previously.

"It's too tight. The second I start to bloat they will once again think I have a baby belly, or tell me I've gained weight, or poke my stomach for a laugh."

"They actually do that?" he asks, horrified.

"Yep. This is why I get so stressed out before these family gatherings. The outfit can't be too loose or too tight. Ooo… I know what would make today fun. Maybe we should play a drinking game. Take a shot anytime someone makes a comment about my body, marriage or babies."

"Christ," he says, running a hand through his hair. "Does it at least help that you're not showing up single this year?"

"It'll help but be prepared for the *when are you going to propose* questions." I wince. "Hopefully though with Gabi and Eric's announcement, the focus will be off me this year."

"I think I can handle it. I just want to make sure you'll be okay."

"I will be. I have to be. I'm doing this for Gabi. At least Nath will be there for the whole of lunch this year. He's always good at trying to keep his mum in check."

I end up settling on a mauve crop and maxi skirt combination. The skirt is tighter around the waist but loose and flowing, not enough to hide a 'baby bump' but loose enough I won't be uncomfortable.

We're packing up everything we need for the lunch, mostly fresh baked goods that Henry and I spent the last few days preparing, when I stop him to give a little extra gift.

"I have one last present for you," I tell him, handing over a small envelope.

"You've already spent enough money on me."

"I didn't spend a cent on this, I promise."

He looks at me sceptically and gently opens the envelope. Inside is a cheap and tacky Christmas card. He opens it up and reads it, and I wring my hands nervously as I wait for him to finish reading. Finally, he finishes and looks down at me, with a look of pure adoration in his eyes.

"Really? Are you sure?" he asks.

"I'm sure. Your rent increase is ridiculous. We've been together for nearly a year, I thought… why not move in together. It makes sense. Don't you think?"

"I do think. I would love to move in with you. I love you, so so much." He sweeps me up into his arms and spins me around the room.

"I love you too." I laugh. "Now put me down. We do not want to be late for this lunch."

***

The moment we arrive at my Aunty Kathy's house, the entire family swarms Henry, asking him question after question. I quickly say hi to my mum and give her a hug, whilst the twins, Tessa and Bridgit, are swooning over Henry's accent and how tall he is. Nath and I stand back and watch it all unfold, laughing. I give it a few minutes before I go in and rescue him.

"Okay, okay, that's enough. Give my man a breather. I'm going to show him around the house. I think Gabi just got here, go hassle her."

I take Henry's hand and take him on a tour, showing him all of the places I played as a kid. I walk him through the backyard and towards the pool.

"I cannot wait to jump into that later. How long do I have to wait?" he asks. A fair question, given its 12pm and already 34 degrees.

"At least until after the main course. My plan is to eat until I feel like I'm going to burst, and then I'm going to sit in that pool floaty to digest," I say, pointing to the pink donut-shaped float.

"Sounds like a perfect plan. Now, should we go and save your sister?"

"Probably. They'll want to start serving food soon, now that everyone has arrived."

We walk back into the house and I steal my sister away from the twins who are following her around like a lost puppy. My sister has always been the twins' idol as they grew up. Anything Gabi did, they did. They absolutely dote on her. I'm the grumpy cousin, they tell me. I give off negative energy, whatever that means. I'm not too worried though – Gabi loves them, but their adoration can be exhausting.

"Lunch is served!" Mum yells from the kitchen, and we all cheer.

"How are you feeling?" Henry asks.

"Not terrible, actually," I tell him. "Maybe having you here will make a difference after all."

"I'm glad."

"Now, are you ready for your first traditional Aussie Christmas feast?" I ask.

He cracks his neck and stretches one arm over the other. "I'm ready. Load me up."

We pile food onto our plates. Mum has done a similar spread to last year: some turkey and ham, and a seafood smorgasbord of baked salmon, prawns, scallops and – much to my disgust, but Henry's delight – oysters. I don't think I've ever seen Henry look so excited about a meal before. His plate is stacked so high I'm worried he's going to lose it all before we get to the table.

We take our seats and I grab us each a beer as we wait for everyone else to join us. Once they do, everyone hands out the Christmas crackers and we all have a turn, the winners putting on their paper hats and reading the jokes out loud. I look to Kathy, who's eyeing my plate as usual. She purses her lips but doesn't say anything this time. *Wow… a Christmas miracle,* I think to myself.

"So, Claudia, you seem happier this Christmas. Do we have this guy to thank for that?" my Uncle Ray says, pointing at Henry with a fork.

"It's been a pretty good year, so yeah, I guess so. We're very happy," I say.

"Agreed," Henry chimes in. "It's been a great year, and with an even better year to come." He takes my hand and kisses my knuckles, eliciting a sigh from the twins.

My mum smiles. "Oh, that's lovely."

"Yeah. Actually, we've got some news—"

"You're pregnant!" Aunty Kathy yells. The table falls silent and Gabi looks across at me, confused.

"No, I'm not pregnant, Kathy. I'm literally drinking a beer right now," I say, taking a massive swig to prove my point.

"You're engaged then!" she says.

"No! Do you see a ring on my finger?" I wave it in front of everyone.

"Oh. Well, what else is there?" she asks.

"Wow. Okay, well Henry is moving in with me. But that's not a ring or a baby so no need to get excited about it." I swallow the lump in my throat. Is the only thing worth making a fuss over a ring or a baby?

"Oh that's wonderful news! Congratulations, you two. That's a huge step in a relationship," says Mum.

"Thank you," I say, a little bit loud and a little bit forceful.

"That's lovely," says Kathy. "How long have you been together now then?"

"It's been almost a year since our first date," Henry tells her.

"So it's a good time to move in then! And uh... when can we expect to see a little bit of bling on that finger, Henry?"

"Mum," Nath warns.

"What? Can't I ask a simple question?" She throws her hands up in innocence. "They're not getting any younger, and if they want to have kids they need to get on it quick sticks."

"Kathy. Stop," Mum interrupts.

"What?" Kathy replies. She looks at me and must register the look of irritation on my face. "I'm just saying, Claudia, you're thirty-three now…"

"We actually have some news!" Gabi stands, interrupting Kathy before she digs herself into a deeper hole.

The whole table turns to look at Gabi, who's holding Eric's hand.

"I – sorry, we – are expecting our first baby in July. I'm pregnant!"

The whole table erupts into cheers and an outpouring of love. Gabi looks over at me and winks. I smile back at her, relieved that she has taken the attention away from me, but also a little bit gutted that my news wasn't celebrated like I had hoped.

"Well…" Henry whispers amongst the chaos. "That was fucking insane."

I laugh. "Yeah. Welcome to my life." I sigh. "You sure you wanna be a part of it?"

"I am one hundred percent in this and nothing will change that. Don't you worry. Are you okay though? That was a lot."

"I'm fine. Kind of. That was pretty bad, but there's been worse. Hopefully now that Gabi's made her announcement, they'll ignore me for the rest of the day."

He leans in and gives me a kiss, and we finish our lunch, listening to the conversations carrying on around us.

I look across the table at Mum and she mouths, *Are you okay?*

I nod and give her a thumbs up. She rolls her eyes at me but laughs. She does her best to reel in her siblings, and I'm grateful for her attempts.

Henry finishes every last thing on his plate, plus three beers. I'm lying with my head on the table, cradling my overstuffed stomach and moaning.

"It's too much. I can't eat another bite," I whinge.

"But Claudia, I made pavlova just for you!" Aunty Amanda says and my head snaps up from the table. They all laugh.

"Never mind," I say. "It appears I have found room for dessert. Henry, you must try the pav. It's the best thing you'll ever eat in your entire life."

"Good thing I have plenty of room then. We make a pretty good *pav,* as you say, back home, so we shall put this to the test," he says, patting his belly.

After helping himself to two whole servings of pavlova, Henry declares that Amanda is the best pavlova chef in the entire world and insists on her teaching him her ways. We're all so full after lunch, and before anyone can make a comment about how bloated my stomach is, I convince Gabi to take a picture of the four of us – her, Eric, Henry and me – with our full bellies, as a great way to announce her pregnancy. We all laugh so hard, and no one dares to make a comment on my body.

We spend the rest of the afternoon swimming in the pool and lazing about in the hot sun. I have a few more beers, and with Henry's company I find myself finally relaxing into the day, the comments at lunch forgotten. By the time it hits 6pm, I'm yawning and ready to curl up on the couch at home. We start to say our goodbyes, but Kathy and Amanda bail me up. Kathy gives me a massive hug, patting me on the back.

"I'm so sorry, love. This must be so hard," she says. *Huh?* I look over her shoulder to Henry, who just shrugs in confusion.

"What's hard?" I ask.

She pulls away from the hug and holds me at arm's length, Amanda coming up next to me to put her arm around my shoulder. "Gabi's pregnancy," Kathy says.

I blink. "What about it?" I don't like where this is going.

"We all know this is what you wanted, Claudia. Marriage and babies. It must be so hard seeing Gabi get it all before you. But you must know that we are here for you, and we understand."

"Your time will come, darling. Don't you worry," Amanda chimes in, looking solemn.

I take a step back, my blood boiling.

"Are you joking?" I demand. "I am nothing but happy for Gabi. I'm so excited to become an aunty."

"It's okay if you're upset, Claudia. It's perfectly normal to feel that way when your younger sister is overshadowing you—"

"Okay, that's enough," Henry interrupts.

The two women turn to look at him.

"Stop making everything a competition between the two sisters. Who cares if Gabi *did it first*. Claudia is happy. She has a wonderful teaching career, she's healthy, she's out there living her best life – a life that I am now lucky enough to be a part of. And all you two are worried about is if she has a ring on her finger or a baby in her womb."

My eyes fill with tears, not from frustration or sadness this time, but from pride.

"That's not all we care about," Kathy says defensively.

"Yes, it is. You didn't ask her a single question today about anything other than marriage or kids. You have to stop. When there is news to share, she will tell you. But right now, I am asking you both to stop." He stands beside me and intertwines his fingers in mine.

"Henry's right," I mumble. "It does feel like that's all you care about. You never ask me about work, or my hobbies or my friends. I told you we were moving in together and you skipped right past it and asked about an engagement ring. I need you to stop. Please."

"Oh. Well, yes of course. We will stop asking questions. Sorry, Claudia." Kathy pats me on the cheek, and the two of them walk away muttering to themselves.

I tip my head back and groan. "Great. Now they're offended and I'll have to be the one to apologise."

"Let it go for today. They can simmer on it for a while. I'm taking you home."

On the car ride home, Henry doesn't let go of my hand. It reminds me of the drive home after the New Year's Eve party, the night we met.

"I understand now, why you hate Christmas," he says. "Having to bear the brunt of that, every year. I'm exhausted after just hearing about it once."

"Yeah. But hey, on the plus side, no one talked about my weight this this year. So… that's a win." I chuckle, but he just holds my hand tighter.

"Thank you," I whisper. "For standing up to them, for standing up for me. I never have the guts to do it. I think I fell even more in love with you tonight."

"I will always stand up for you. You won't ever have to worry about that. I'm just sorry your Christmas was ruined. Again."

"It's fine. Like I said, I'm used to it."

We drive the rest of the way home in silence, Christmas carols playing softly on the radio and a few tears spilling down my cheeks. We pull up into the driveway and Henry turns the car off and faces me. "Tonight, I make a promise to you."

"Okay…"

"I promise to make you fall in love with Christmas again. By December next year, you will be so excited for Christmas you'll feel like a kid again."

I rest my head against the headrest and let out a sigh. I'm tired, and so glad this day is over. But I'm also sad, because this man right here deserves to have the best Christmases, and he won't get that dating me.

"You're sweet, Henry, but I don't think that's going to happen."

He smirks and unclicks my seatbelt, dragging me over the centre console and onto his lap. He kisses me slow and deep, taking my breath and stress away with the sweep of his tongue. Pulling back, he rests his forehead on mine.

"Watch me."

PART THREE

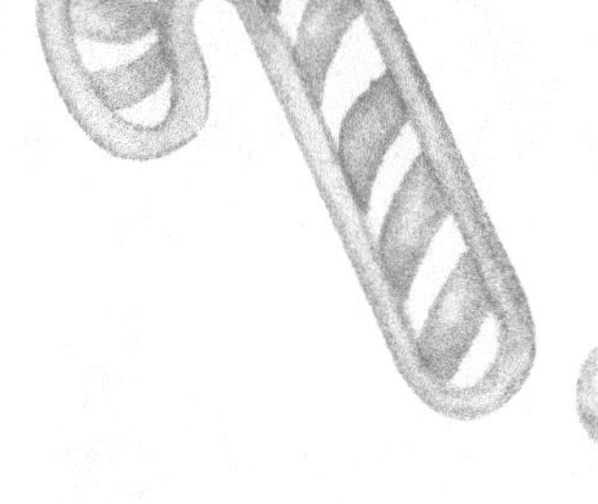

ELEVEN
First Attempt

"Will you please tell me where we are going?" I ask Henry.

"No. That defeats the purpose of a surprise, Claudia."

We've been driving in the car for just over an hour, heading who knows where. When Henry told me he was taking me away for a weekend surprise, I was both excited and scared. I hate surprises, something he should have realised by now. He wouldn't even let me pack my own bag.

"Fine," I mumble. "You know I hate surprises."

"I know. That's why I do it, to see you unravel. You get the cutest little frown line when you're stressed," he teases.

I roll my eyes at him and he grabs my hand and rests it on his leg. We sit like that for the rest of the drive, listening to my old school emo playlist that I curated with the likes of Good Charlotte, My Chemical Romance and All Time Low. After another forty minutes, we pull into a dirt driveway – it's long, and about half way we see a sign that reads *Day Break Farm Stay*.

"A farm stay?" I ask, voice pitched.

Henry grins. "Yep."

"Oh my god. Do they have…"

"Highland cows? Yes. Yes they do."

The noise that comes out of me is barely human. I *love* Highland cows. I've never seen one in real life but I have many portraits of them around my house. I knew there were farms around South Australia that had some, and I've been meaning to book in for a visit, but this…

"Babe, I could cry right now."

"You're welcome." He chuckles. "That's not the only surprise I have in store though."

We pull up in front of a gorgeous farm style cottage, alongside two other cars that I immediately recognise. I jump out of the car as Nath, Frankie, Oliver, Eric, Gabi and my brand-new baby nephew all file out of the house.

"Surprise!" they yell in unison.

"What the hell? What are you guys doing here?" My eyes well up as I go around and hug each of them.

"Merry Christmas in July weekend!" Nath says, looking smug.

"Christmas in July?" My brows knit in confusion.

"Yes. Christmas in July. Operation 'Make Claudia fall in love with Christmas again' starts now," Henry says, walking up behind me with our bags.

I turn to glare at him, but I can't stop the grin from spreading across my face.

"I want to tell you it's not going to work but… this is the nicest thing anyone has ever done for me. Thank you."

At that moment, Cooper, my nephew, decides it's feeding time and starts to get fussy.

"And you, Gabi, what the hell are you guys doing here? You gave birth four weeks ago!"

"So? I've recovered pretty well, given how quickly he came out. Not a tear in sight by some miracle."

"Don't need to hear that!" Nath sing-songs.

"Deal with it!" she yells back. "I didn't think I was going to make it when Henry first told me about the plans, but since this one decided to arrive a month early, I thought why not? I mostly wanted to come so I could see your face when you found out this was a Christmas-inspired weekend." She grins.

"Yeah, yeah. Now give me my little smooch, I've missed him." I reach for the baby, but he starts to cry.

"Once he's fed, he's all yours."

We walk into the cottage, and it's so beautiful I want to move in immediately. Hardwood floors run throughout, with rugs thoughtfully scattered to add an extra layer of comfort. A large farm-style dining table of reclaimed wood sits in the middle of the room, with bench seating to fit at least ten people. A chandelier bathes the space in a soft glow, creating the perfect atmosphere for relaxing. There's a fully equipped kitchen, and past that is the hallway leading to the bedrooms. But the biggest feature of the house is the large stone fireplace in the living area. A fire is already roaring, the flicker of the flames and soft crackling of the wood instantly calming me. There's just something about an open fireplace that makes me feel at home.

We head down the hallway towards the main bedroom. Henry had offered it to Gabi and Eric but they insisted we take it as it was my surprise weekend. Inside the room is a very comfortable looking king-sized bed, facing floor to ceiling windows that overlook one of the paddocks. Attached to the bedroom is an ensuite, with a large open shower and complete with a clawfoot tub.

"Wow," I breathe. "I never want to leave this place."

"I'm glad you like it."

"I know I said it earlier, but really, thank you. This is exactly what I need."

"You're most welcome. Now, are you ready for step one?"

"Step one of…?"

"Operation 'Make Claudia Fall in love with Christmas'."

I groan. "I guess I don't really have much of a choice, do I?"

"Nope. Not at all. I made you a promise last Christmas and I intend to see it through."

"Fine. What's step one?"

"Decorating!"

He opens up one of the bags and it contains a multitude of Christmas decorations, including tinsel, baubles, stockings and lights.

"I also have this. You are required to wear it when participating in all Christmas-themed activities."

He pulls out two matching Christmas jumpers. His jumper has my face all over it, and my jumper has his face all over it.

"They're custom-made," he says proudly.

"I can see that." I laugh. "I really want to hate them, but I actually love them. One point served to you."

I take the jumper from him and put it on, then I head back into the living room to decorate. Frankie has started playing Christmas carols over the built in speaker and Nath has started making mulled wine on the stove. Cooper is asleep in Eric's arms and Gabi is pumping. Henry joins me and puts his arm around my waist.

"Is this what it's supposed to be like?" I ask.

"Relaxing and carefree? Surrounded by people who love you and want the best for you with no hidden meanings or intentions? Yeah. This is what it's supposed to feel like."

I nuzzle into his side, and he places a kiss on the top of my head.

"Alright, let's Christma-fy this bitch!" Frankie yells. "Nice jumpers, losers." She winks at me and proceeds to pull on her own matching Christmas jumper with Oliver's face on it. It seems everyone has the same matching jumper with their partner, except Nath, who has Cooper's chubby round head featuring on his.

Everyone has brought a bag of Christmas decorations, and soon the cottage is full of twinkling lights, stockings are hung up on the fireplace mantle, and we even have a Christmas tree – thanks to Oliver, who managed to stuff one in the boot of his car. The large pot of mulled wine is now gently simmering on the stove, creating a deliciously sweet and spicy aroma through-out the whole house. I pour myself a cup and sit on the floor next to the fireplace, taking in everything happening around me and feeling a sense of contentment.

"God, I wish we had a wintery Christmas like in the northern hemisphere. This is what it should be like," I tell the group.

"Agreed," says Gabi.

"Have you ever had a White Christmas?" asks Oliver.

"Never. It's on the bucket list though, maybe one day. Perhaps this one can take me home one year so I can tick it off." I gesture to Henry, and he winks at me.

"That would be so fun," Nath says. "Oh, I almost forgot to ask. Did your long service leave get approved?"

"It did! After ten years, I'm finally taking some time off. I'm more excited than I thought I would be, actually."

"Which is hilarious, given how much convincing it took you to even apply for it. I practically had to send the application myself," says Henry.

"Yeah well, you all know what I'm like. I still have no idea how I'm going to fill in my time. October to January is a huge break."

"I'm sure you'll find something to do," says Frankie.

Henry's phone dings with a text and he immediately breaks into a smile as he reads it. "That was the owner of the farm. They're about to feed the cows and have asked if we'd like to help."

I've never gotten up off the floor so fast in my entire life.

"I'll take that as a yes," he laughs.

We all put our shoes back on and head out through the back door, towards the paddock we saw the cows in earlier. It's been raining this week, and the mud squelches underneath my boots.

"I apologise in advance if I cry," I tell the group.

"They're just cows," Gabi says.

"You just don't get me," I say dramatically.

We make our way over to the where the farmers are standing with a bundle of hay, surrounded by six highland cows, two of which are calves.

"Okay. I'm crying. I didn't know there would be babies!" Tears well in my eyes as I take tentative steps towards them, not wanting to freak them out.

"I hear you're a fan?" says the older male farmer.

"A slight fan," Henry tells him.

"Want to feed the calves?"

"It would only be a dream come true! What do I need to do?"

He shows me how to hold the hay in my hand, palm flat, and then instructs me to hold my arm out and wait for them to come to me. It doesn't take long, and both calves are munching the hay straight out of my hand, faster than I can replenish it. They start bumping their nose into my legs and rubbing themselves up against me.

"Can I pat them too?" I ask.

"Of course," the farmer says. "They're very friendly."

I rub my hand on the head of the smallest calf, and my face feels like it'll break from smiling. I hear the snap of a camera shutter and look over at Henry, who's taking photos on the old film camera. His smile is as big as mine, until one of the bigger cows bumps into him from behind and he almost falls over into the mud.

"This is incredible," I tell him. Looking around, the others are enjoying themselves as much as I am. Nath keeps tickling Frankie on the back of the neck with the hay and Oliver is poking the cow patties. Gabi and Eric are taking selfies with Cooper and the cows, even though he's only four weeks old and has no clue what is going on, but it's a core memory for all of us.

We take so many photos, and the cows are so friendly that I end up giving them all big smooches on their heads. Once they're all fed, the farmer leads them away to where they rest for the evening, and we all head back into the house to start dinner, hearts full.

***

Our 'Christmas Dinner' consists of a roast lamb, crispy roast potatoes, pumpkin and carrots, beans and peas, a couple of side salads, fresh bread rolls (courtesy of Henry) and my famous gravy. It's so delicious, and I eat so much I end up changing into my pyjama pants for more comfort.

"What's for dessert?" Frankie chirps.

We all groan. I've never seen anyone who can put away food like Frankie.

"Dessert is more of an activity," Henry says. "We're making gingerbread houses. You can eat as much or as little as you want."

He proceeds to pull multiple Tupperware containers out of nowhere, filled with freshly baked gingerbread pieces, ready to assemble into little houses.

"When did you bake all of this?" I ask.

"Shelly gave me free range of the kitchen on Thursday."

"I thought I could smell ginger in your hair when you came home," I say, and he laughs.

We all create little stations on the big dining table and get to work. Henry has thought of everything: he's whipped up the icing, provided so many different shades of food colouring, sprinkles, lollies, glitter… the works. My heart warms at all of the effort he has put into making this weekend the Christmas of my dreams, even if it isn't really Christmas.

"This is already the best Christmas I've had in years, and it's not even December," I tell the group while we're focussing on our creations.

"I admit," Nath starts, "I've felt more Christmas spirit today than I have in years."

Gabi nods. "I hate to say it out loud, but the fact that I'm enjoying myself so much and our family *isn't* here, kinda says a lot."

"I was thinking the same thing," Nath says.

"I love our family, I do, but they really kill the vibes some-times," says Gabi.

"Maybe this is what we need to do," Nath suggests. "Start our own Christmas traditions. We're old enough now, we can do our own thing."

The guilt in me starts to rear its ugly head, and the roast lamb in my stomach starts to churn at the thought.

"You mean, skip Christmas with everyone?" I ask. Henry senses my hesitation and nudges me with his foot under the table.

"Not skip it entirely. We can have a Christmas dinner on Christmas Eve, or Boxing Day, or whenever. And then on Christmas day, we do our own thing. No family pressure, no shitty comments, no rude comments about our bodies… it would be what we want it to be."

"That actually sounds perfect," Gabi chimes in, looking at Eric. "Now that we have Cooper, the idea of having to drag him around to three separate Christmases makes me nauseous. We could start our own traditions."

The idea in theory sounds perfect, and I want to say yes. But the people pleaser in me is screaming, *'How dare you abandon your family on Christmas day!'*

"I dunno, guys. I can just hear them all now. It's hard enough having to choose each year which family to spend the day with." I chew on my bottom lip, thinking of how it could pos-sibly work.

"So pick no one, easy fix!" Nath says. "Honestly, it's just a day. Does it really matter?"

"Everyone keeps saying it's just a day, and yet when it comes to the actual day, someone is always disappointed and makes me feel bad."

Nath's eyes soften. "I know, Claud. It's just an idea, some-thing to think about. You've got about four months before they start to ask about Christmas, so you have time."

Henry shifts in his chair, and the others offer me smiles in support. They understand – they may not feel exactly the way I do, but they understand.

"Thanks, guys. I'll think about it."

We continue building our gingerbread houses, sipping on mulled wine and snacking on the off cuts. There're multiple curses from everyone across the table when the structural integrity of the houses fail, and cheers of delight when they're finally finished. We all take it in turns explaining our creations and naming them, before voting on the winner.

"No fair," I whinge. "You're a professional baker. I think it's unfair for you to win."

Henry kisses my pout and laughs. "Sore loser."

We retreat to the couches and stay up for the rest of the night, telling stories of our childhoods, laughing at memories and embracing the new ones we are making. Eventually, when no one can keep their eyes open any longer, we retreat into our bedrooms.

I'm curled up in bed with Henry, and he's rubbing my back in soothing circles.

"Did you have a good day?" he asks.

"The best day," I tell him. "This has been the best Christmas I've had in a long time."

"Did it work? Have I reinvigorated your love for Christmas?" he asks, hopeful.

I consider it. If Christmas could be like this every year, I would love it. Then I remember the conversation at dinner, and the idea to create our own traditions and skip the family Christmas, and the guilt sinks in once more.

"I don't know. Maybe, but I think we'll have to see how this year goes."

"I'll keep on trying then."

"I know you will."

We lie there in silence for a little while longer. I feel Henry place a kiss on my forehead before I fall into a blissful, uninterrupted sleep.

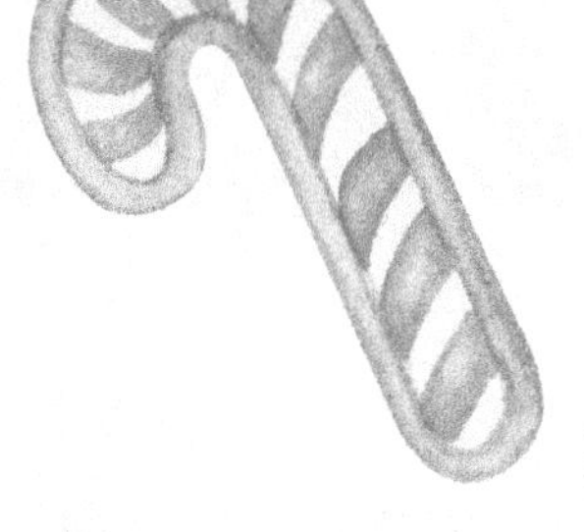

TWELVE
Birthday

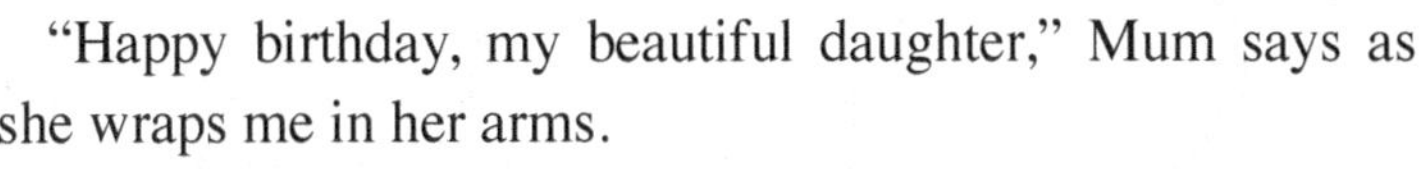

"Happy birthday, my beautiful daughter," Mum says as she wraps me in her arms.

"Thanks, Mum."

"Happy birthday, Claud," Dad says.

"Thanks, Dad." I reach over and give him a hug.

My birthday is the only time of year that my parents put aside their differences and come together to celebrate me. We're out for dinner – so they can't argue in public – along with Gabi, Eric and this year, Henry. It's the beginning of the September school holidays, and I'm now officially on long service leave for the first time in my career. I have seventeen weeks off work and have absolutely no idea how I'm going to spend my time.

We've decided to come back to Jimmies, because they really do make the best cocktails and it has become a bit of a go to venue for celebrations. The weather is warming up, changing from the dreary South Australian cold to the perfect spring temperature, so we're sitting in the beer garden among the fairy lights and greenery. Gabi and Eric rock up,

Cooper still asleep in his pram. I give them all a hug and fawn over my baby nephew, until Gabi smacks me away so I don't wake him.

"Have you had a good day?" Mum asks.

"I have. Henry treated me to a beautiful breakfast at the bakery, and then we went for a hike up Mount Lofty. It's been a gorgeous day."

"And what did he get you for your birthday?" Dad winks.

"Absolutely nothing," I tease.

"Yet," Henry butts in. "I was waiting until tonight to give you your gift."

Mum gasps a little.

"Relax, Mum, he's not proposing. We've talked about that." I roll my eyes.

"Sorry, sorry. I know we did." She looks down sheepishly.

Henry and I have actually been avoiding the conversation about our future. There's still so much uncertainty. He told me when we first met that he only planned on being here for two years, and those two years are up in December. He doesn't have a ticket to fly home yet, but he needs to make a decision and book it soon if he's to stick to his original plan.

I don't think either of us expected to fall in love so fast and so hard. He's unlike any man I've ever met. I know we both want the same things in life, we just permanently reside on opposite sides of the world. I know we have to talk about it soon. I just keep avoiding it, because if my history is anything to go by, it will probably end in heartbreak.

Henry and I lock eyes and I smile at him, trying to hide the dread within me. He sees it though, of course he does, and he kisses my knuckles in reassurance.

Gabi clears her throat, breaking the awkwardness of the moment, and my parents give me my present. Apparently I'm super hard to buy for, because they all get me a gift voucher. One for a camping and hiking store, one for a couples Thai cooking class, and the other for one of my favourite book stores, *Fiction and Friction*.

"My turn," Henry says nervously, and hands me a small gift bag.

I open it up and take out the tissue paper inside. What I find confuses me a little bit. I pull out a red and white scarf with 'CANADA' written in all caps, complete with a maple leaf.

"It's… lovely. Thank you, babe. I'll represent your country with pride."

He laughs. "That's not the only part of the gift," he starts. "I know you've been trying to think of something to do during your long service leave."

"I have," I say sceptically.

"Well, I think I've come up with a solution, at least for a few weeks. Open the envelope."

I look inside the bag and see there is in fact a small envelope. Opening it, I take out the folded piece of paper, frowning in confusion.

"Henry… what is this?"

"This… is your flight to Ontario. I'm taking you home for Christmas." He tucks a stray hair behind my ear, and I burst into tears.

Mum's hand flies to cover her mouth, completely overjoyed, and Dad leans back in his chair, chuckling to himself. Gabi smiles mischievously and Eric nods, raising his glass at Henry.

"Did I do good?" he whispers, pulling me into his arms.

"Henry, this is way too much," I sob into his shirt.

"No it's not. I know we haven't talked about it, but I want to take you home to meet my family, before we make any decision about our future. I've been planning this for a while, actually."

I lean back to look at him, makeup smudged and tears dampening my cheeks. "Is this why you were so persistent on me taking leave this term?" I ask.

"Maybe," he says cheekily. "I had some backup."

I look over at Gabi and glare at her. She's grinning ear to ear.

"You were also very insistent on me taking this term off. You knew."

"Of course I knew. You weren't going to take the time off without a decent push, and I didn't want you to ruin Henry's plans." She shrugs.

I look over at my parents, who are lit up with delight. "I didn't know," Mum says, tears lining eyes.

"Neither did I," Dad adds. "You're going to Canada, kiddo."

I turn back to Henry. "This is insane."

"No, it's perfect," he says.

"Are you sure you guys are okay with me being gone for Christmas?" I ask, turning specifically to Dad. "I was supposed to spend it with you this year, and now I'm skipping it. Again."

"Claudia, what have I always said about Christmas?" he asks. I don't answer him. "It's just a day. We can celebrate it on any day. We can celebrate in March for all I care." He takes my hand and gives it a squeeze. "It's just a day."

I look at Mum. "What he said," she replies, gesturing to Dad.

I turn back to Henry and grin. "I guess I'm going to Canada for Christmas."

He smiles back, grabbing my face with both hands and smooching me.

My parents laugh and look at each other, then scowl. I roll my eyes but let it go. Nothing can ruin this moment for me.

"I can't believe I'm going to Canada. Wait, does it snow at Christmas?" I ask.

"Most years it does. I think they're predicting quite the snow-fall this year," Henry tells me.

"Something to tick off the bucket list. You're getting a White Christmas!" Gabi squeals.

"I'm glad I got you that voucher, Claud," Dad adds. "I think you're going to need to go shopping for some snow gear."

"You're not wrong. I have one jacket, I think."

"Yeah, pre-warning, it gets *cold,*" Henry says.

"I don't really care," I tell them. "I'm so excited. I want to see everything. Do your parents know we're coming?"

"They're the ones who suggested it, actually. They've been dying to meet you in person."

"When do we leave?"

"November twentieth. So you still have a couple of months to relax at home before we go."

"Like I'm going to be able to relax, knowing this. I'm not going to be able to sleep until we leave."

"Phase two of my plan is in motion." He winks.

"Oh, so you think whisking me away to another country is going to make me fall in love with Christmas again, do you?" I tease.

"I do. If you don't love Christmas by the end of this trip, I will eat that scarf."

I wrap the scarf around my neck and wink at him. "Game on."

THIRTEEN
Flying Home

"Have you got everything?"

"I think so," I reply, going over the list once more.

Passport? Check. Charger? Check. Hand sanitiser? Check. Latest Katherine Center novel? Check.

"Why am I so nervous all of a sudden?" I say to Henry.

"Probably because we're about to be flying for around twenty-five hours. And you're going to meet my parents, properly, for the first time tomorrow."

"Oh yeah. That's probably it. And… you know, I hope they like me," I say, somewhat sarcastically.

Henry rolls his eyes. "We've been video calling with them at least once a week for almost a year. They love you."

"Yeah, through a screen. What if I'm different in real life? What if I smell or something?"

I get a deadpan look in response and bite my lip to stop myself from laughing too hard.

"Very funny," Henry says. "They're so excited to see you."

"And you. They're finally getting their baby back." *Maybe for good,* I think to myself. We both have a return flight for early January, but he could change his mind once he's home.

"It will be good to see them, that's for sure. Alright, your mum just pulled up outside. Ready to go?" he asks.

"All set."

We wheel our suitcases toward Mum's car. She kindly offered to take us to the airport, despite it being six o'clock in the morning.

"Ready to go then?" she asks.

"Sure am. Thanks again for doing this, Mum. I really appreciate it."

"I wouldn't have it any other way."

She opens the boot of her car and we load the cases inside. Henry pats his jacket pocket and his pants.

"I think I have everything. You guys hop in the car and I'll do one last check and lock up the house," he tells us.

We get in the car and Mum turns the radio down.

"How are you feeling? Nervous? Excited?"

"All of the above," I admit.

"Have you talked about what happens after?" she asks, looking towards the front door of the house.

"Well, we both have a return ticket back home, so that's a good sign. I think it will all depend on what happens on the trip. If he gets the urge to move back home…" I swallow back my panic.

"Don't even think about that, Claudia. He loves you, most ardently, in the words of Mr. Darcy." I laugh at that. "If he wants to move back home, he will tell you."

I sigh. "You're right. I have to remain hopeful. He makes me so happy, I'm so afraid to lose him," I whisper that last part.

"I know. But if I'm correct, and I usually am, you two are destined to be together. Opposing continents be damned."

"Thanks, Mum. I'll hold onto that."

I see Henry lock and close the front door, then jiggle it about ten times to make sure it's properly secure, before he heads back towards the car with a big grin on his face.

"We are all ready to depart!" he yells as he opens the door.

"Let's get you two on a plane then, shall we?"

…

"I'm so bored," I whinge in Henry's ear.

"Sorry sweetheart, we still have…" he checks the flight tracker on the screen in front of him. "… two and a half hours to go until we land."

I whimper at the thought. I feel like we've been on this plane forever. My feet are swollen, my butt is numb, my skin feels so dry, despite the copious amounts of water I've been guzzling down.

"Do you want to watch a movie together?" he asks.

"Well, I've finished my book so we might as well. What do you want to watch?"

He spends a few minutes perusing the collection of movies on the screen before choosing *Pride and Prejudice*. I rear back in my seat and look at him, shocked.

"What?" he asks.

"You want to watch *Pride and Prejudice*?"

"Yes, it's a brilliant movie. Do you not want to?"

"Of course I do, I would never say no. It's funny, Mum quoted Mr. Darcy in the car. I can't believe we've been together for nearly two years and I had absolutely no idea you liked this movie."

He shrugs. "I guess there are still some things to learn about each other. Now come on, get yours set up so we can watch at the same time, or we'll have to turn it off before the cold hands scene."

I chuckle in surprise and find the movie on the screen. We press play at the same time and I put my headphones on, snuggle up tight with my standard issue blanket and rest my head on Henry's shoulder. I fall asleep right as Charles moves back to London and only wake when the pilot announces we are making our descent, missing almost the entire film.

***

"HENRY!"

We turn our heads in the direction of a woman screaming.

"Henry!"

Henry waited for me as I passed through the foreign visitor line, so we could walk to baggage collection together and meet his parents. We're heading towards the baggage carousel when the crowd in front of us clears and a short, older woman with a blonde bob and an older man with salt and pepper hair are standing with a huge sign and smiling from ear to ear. The sign reads 'Welcome home Henry and Claudia… for now!'

Henry beams and throws his head back and laughs before beelining for his parents. They wrap him up in a huge embrace as I stand awkwardly to the side, until his mum, whose grip is stronger than I anticipated, pulls me into the group hug.

"Claudia, I am so happy to finally meet you." Henry's mum, Lori, steps back and holds me at arm's length so she can see me properly. She has a certain air about her, one that immediately makes me feel at ease.

"I'm happy to be here," I tell her, unsure why tears start to line my eyes.

"Oh no, none of that now, or you'll set me off," she says, hugging me again.

Henry and his dad, Walter, are hugging next to me, and then we swap, his dad wrapping me up in a hug so tight he nearly cuts off my air supply.

"I can see where Henry gets his height from," I wheeze. He pulls back, realising he's slowly starving me of oxygen, and laughs.

"Yes, one of the many traits he picked up from me. I'm glad you're both here." He turns back to Henry. "Your mother has been planning non-stop for weeks now."

"Of course I have, Walt. I've missed my boy." She pats Henry on the cheek tenderly. "And I've been dying to hug this lovely lady in person. Now, let's collect your bags so we can be on our way. We have a short drive home and then you two can have a shower and relax by the fire. How does that sound?"

"Sounds perfect to me. I don't even know what time it is or what day it is. Where are we again?"

Henry laughs. "Ottawa airport. It is currently 3:10pm, on Wednesday the nineteenth of November."

"That was a rhetorical question. Mostly," I muse.

"I know." He winks.

We grab our bags off of the carousel and make our way to the car. I swear when we first walk outside, forgetting that it was going to be cold. When we left Adelaide, it was a sunny 29 degrees. Leaving the airport terminal, Lori tells me that it's currently negative one. I packed my thick coat in my carry on, and I'm glad I thought to dig it out before walking out of the terminal doors.

"Have you had much snow yet, Mum?" Henry asks.

"Some, but not enough to stick to the ground for very long. They're predicting quite the snowy December, so I think it's a pretty safe bet that you'll get your White Christmas, Claudia."

"Sounds great," I say through chattering teeth. "That gives me about a month to climatise so I can actually enjoy it."

They all laugh at me, the poor cold Australian girl, as we pile into the family car. It's about a forty-minute drive from the airport to Almonte, and I spend the whole time staring out of the window and soaking in the landscape surrounding me. Henry holds my hand for the entirety of the drive, and when we arrive at his home town, a small frown starts to form between my brows.

"Why does this place look so familiar?" I ask to no one in particular.

I feel as though we're driving onto the set of a Christmas film. The streets are lined with old historic buildings, adorned with garlands and twinkling lights. There appears to have been a light dusting of snow throughout the day, and locals walk along the paths, most likely conducting their Christmas shopping.

"How many Christmas films have you watched?" Walter asks.

"Uhh…" I hesitate. "A few."

Henry snickers.

"Shush, you. I told you, I love everything about Christmas, except for Christmas itself. What do Christmas movies have to do with anything?"

"Well, Almonte has been the filming location for quite a few Hallmark Christmas films. As you can see, it's the perfect location for it."

I gasp. "No way. I'm a huge sucker for Hallmark movies. God, no wonder you are the way you are," I say, gesturing to Henry.

"What's that supposed to mean?" he asks.

"You literally grew up in a Christmas town. Of course you love Christmas so much."

"Henry used to be one of Santa's elves growing up." Lori smirks.

"Oh my god… please tell me you have pictures."

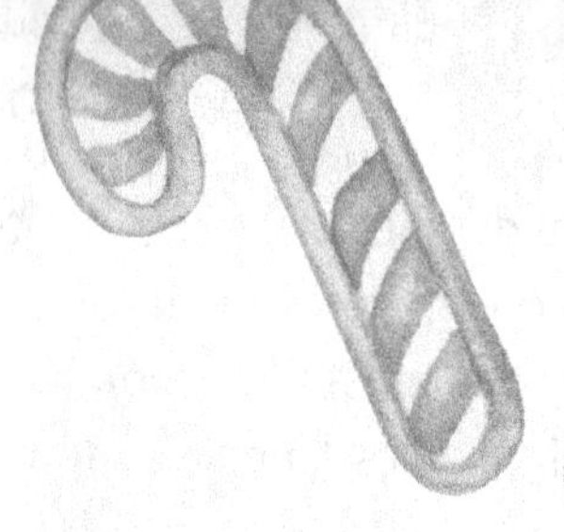

FOURTEEN
Sugar and Whisk

A few days after we arrive, it's Lori's birthday, and we've booked into her favourite restaurant in town for dinner to celebrate – *The Stirling*.

"I've already looked up the menu," I tell Henry. "I'm excited, now that the jetlag has finally worn off I am ready to be fully functional again."

It has taken me so long to get over my jetlag. I didn't think it would be this bad, but I've had to nap every day since we landed, and I've barely made it through dinner each night before collapsing into bed and sleeping for twelve hours. I even fell asleep standing up, just like Henry did in the bathroom on the first day we met. Today is the first day I've felt human since we arrived, so I'm keen to finally explore the town properly.

"Of course you've looked up the menu already," he chuckles. "I could have predicted that. Before we do anything else today though, we have to go to the bakery and make Mum's birthday cupcakes."

"Oh, I can't wait to see it," I say dreamily.

"It's closed today, so I'll get to give you the full private tour." He winks.

"Does this tour include samples of any and or all items I desire?"

"Perhaps."

"Then what are we waiting for?" I jump up to put on my coat and scarf, as Henry laughs behind me.

"Don't forget your toque," he says.

"My what?"

"Your toque. This right here." He pulls my beanie off of the coat rack and plonks it on my head.

"You mean my beanie," I chuckle. "I've never heard of a toque."

"Welcome to Canada." He smirks, putting on his own layers.

One thing I still haven't gotten used to is the cold, and how many layers of clothing I'm required to wear. The constant routine of having to put clothes on and off and on again is exhausting. Adelaide winters usually require a coat at most. Here, I've got thermals on, boots, gloves, a scarf, beanie and a coat. It takes me ten minutes just to get going anywhere.

I don my winter gear and we head out the front door. The weather is turning it on for us today – it's still bitterly cold but there's also a little bit of sun peeking through the clouds. It's been snowing lightly for the last few days, and the streets are dusted with a fine white powder. It really is quite beautiful, that is, until I fall on my arse three times on the black ice coating the roads.

"I'm not built for this," I mutter to Henry as he helps me stand up after the third fall.

"I told you to buy better boots for this trip," he reminds me.

"Yeah well, I thought these would be good enough." I gesture to my old Dr Martins.

"Should have listened to me," he teases.

"Yeah, yeah, whatever. I'll go buy some tomorrow. Now, what were you saying about this Christmas festival?"

"Well, there are a few different events that are held leading up to Christmas, and the first one is on December sixth. It's called Light Up the Night. Basically it's one big street party with food and music, and Santa pays a visit."

"Oh, that actually sounds pretty great. So is it kind of like an official launch of Christmas?"

"You could say that. The parade usually follows a few days after. You think it's Christmassy here now, just wait until the first of December."

For the first time in years, decades even, I start to feel a tingle of excitement for Christmas. We've spent a week with Henry's family and there have been zero comments about marriage or pregnancy, and no comments about my weight or how much I'm eating.

"I'm looking forward to it," I say shyly.

He notices my quiet tone and reaches out to hold my hand as we walk along the footpath, heading into the main street of town. It's a quick ten-minute walk from Henry's home and it feels good to be outside in the crisp, fresh air.

The cold stings my cheeks and I have a soft red flush on my face by the time we arrive at the Cambell Family bakery, *Sugar and Whisk*. The bakery is situated in an old stone single-story building. There's a bay window at the front, decorated with bows and a pine Christmas garland. Christmas lights twinkle along the window frame, a huge wreath hangs on the front door and a welcome mat that says *'Hello, Sugar!'* greets everyone who enters.

Henry unlocks the door and I am immediately met with the lingering smell of baked treats. There's a hint of ginger in the air due to the enormous amounts of gingerbread they've been baking lately. The room itself is adorned in silver, white and pink Christmas decorations. Tinsel wraps around the checkout counter, and above it hangs baubles of varying sizes. Each of the white vintage tables is decorated with a wood-carved reindeer, more tinsel and a sprig of holly. A large Christmas tree sits in one corner next to the bay window, which houses a booth seat overlooking the main street. Small frames hang on the walls with paintings of cakes and cookies and pastries, as well as a wall of family portraits of the Cambell Family. Henry's photo is the latest addition, and he's smiling proudly.

"Henry, this place is adorable." We both take off our coats, scarves and hats, hanging them on the coat rack by the door.

"It's my second home." He smiles softly, taking in the decorations his mum so lovingly put up. He walks up behind me and wraps his arms around my waist, resting his chin atop my head. "You like it?"

"I love it."

"Look up."

I do, and hanging above us is a sprig of mistletoe, tied together with a pink ribbon. I gasp.

"Mistletoe!"

"You know what happens when you stop under mistletoe?" he asks.

I spin in his arms and grab his face with both hands, pulling him to me with such force he lets out a laugh as our mouths collide. He kisses me with a smile, as I pull on his hair and bite his bottom lip.

I grin when I pull away. "Mistletoe isn't really a thing back home. I've always wanted to do that."

"Happy to be your first. Hopefully your first of many." He winks. "Now, would you like to see where the magic happens?"

"Lead the way."

He takes my hand and walks me behind the counter and through a swinging door that leads to the bakery kitchen. In the middle of the room is a long, wooden prep table, with wooden posts attaching it to the ceiling. Along one side is a bench that holds all of the equipment required for baking. There are two large ovens on the opposite wall, along with a proofer and industrial sized mixer. At the back of the room is the walk-in refrigerator and next to it, the pantry. There are shelves going up the walls containing baking sheets and cake pans, measuring cups and mixing bowls. It's all so neat and tidy, but also quaint enough that it doesn't feel cold. Small arch windows let in natural light, and the timber beams on the ceiling mixed with the stone walls gives it more of a cottage bakehouse feel.

"So this is where you spent your childhood, huh?"

"Sure is. This is where I learnt it all. My mum and my nana used to bring me to work before and after school. I helped out with serving customers once I was old enough, and then eventually asked if I could be taught how to bake. My nana passed when I was fifteen, but not before she taught me some of her secret recipes." He smiles fondly at the memory.

"You must truly love it," I say.

"I do. It's all I've ever known, but I wouldn't have it any other way. Some people spend their lives resenting the family business and the expectation to take over, but I've always been so excited by it."

I clear my throat and swallow down my worry, the complexities of our relationship rising to the surface once again.

"So," I start, changing the subject. "What are we making today?"

"Red velvet cupcakes and chocolate chip cookies. Mum's favourite. I thought we could try your recipe."

"Okay, sounds good."

Henry preheats the ovens and gets out all of the ingredients and tools we need. He sets out making the batter for the cupcakes, while I prepare the cookie dough. My main ingredient that I use in my cookies is hot chocolate powder. It adds an extra element of chocolatey goodness without being too overpowering. I roughly chop up the chocolate pieces, stealing a few samples along the way. We prep the icing, a delicious soft pink butter cream with edible glitter mixed in.

"You've got something on your pants," Henry says, pointing to the back of my pants.

I turn my head to look, when suddenly he smacks my arse

with both hands, leaving floury hand prints behind. I yelp and run away from him laughing. Glaring at him from the opposite side of the table, I grab a fistful of flour from the huge bag.

"Don't do it," he warns.

I raise my arm higher, ready to throw. He grins the most devilish of grins and starts to circle the table, trying to get behind me. I start to run but feign right and turn at the last minute to throw flour at him. It hits him in the side of the face, dusting his hair and stubble. I laugh so hard tears prick my eyes as he swoops me up in his arms and shakes his head, showering me in flour.

"You are trouble," he murmurs in my ear, and then bites my earlobe, causing me to shriek.

"You started it," I laugh.

"I'd say we're even." He gives me a quick kiss on the tip of my nose and puts me down.

"We should probably finish these off so they can go in the oven," I tell him.

Once the batter and dough are done, we pour the cupcakes into patty-pans and roll out the dough into small balls on the baking tray. We place the cookies in one oven, and the cupcakes in the other. Henry sets a timer and then looks at me with a fire in his eyes.

"So… what do you want to do while we wait?" he asks.

"Um… we should probably clean up." I gesture to the bench and floor, now coated in flour.

He shakes his head. "Try again."

"Keep an eye on the food so it doesn't burn?"

He shakes his head again. "Claudia. Come here."

He crooks a finger at me and I come to him as if being pulled by an invisible string. I reach him, and he walks me backward, slowly, until my lower back hits the wooden bench. I crane my neck to look up at him, and he gives me a look that sends my heart racing and my knees quivering.

Leaning down, he kisses me, moaning into my mouth as he tastes the sweetness of the chocolate I'd been pilfering. Lifting me effortlessly, he sits me atop the bench, my back resting against one of the carved wooden posts. I wrap my legs around his waist and pull him closer, desperate to feel him against me.

"There aren't any cameras in here, are there?" I ask, slightly out of breath.

"None," he says, stepping back so he can lift my jumper above my head. He growls in frustration when he discovers a second layer, my thermals, and I laugh as he struggles to take them off gracefully. He reaches for my jeans, undoes the button and pulls down the zip, swiftly tugging them from my hips, only to discover another set of thermals. He gives me a *what the hell is this* look.

I laugh. "It's really cold today."

He makes quick work of pulling them off and finally has me sitting in just my underwear and bra. He softly kisses my neck, sending shivers down my spine and making me heady with need. Reaching behind me, he unclasps my bra, leaving my breasts exposed. The heat from the ovens takes the chill out of the room, but my nipples peak anyway from the anticipation of what's to come. I reach for his jumper and tug it off over his head, running my hands down his stomach and below his belt. I can feel his hardness through his jeans and I'm suddenly desperate for him to be inside me.

"Take these off," I pant.

"Not yet," he says, nuzzling into my neck.

Dropping to his knees in front of me, he spreads my legs wide open, kissing the soft spot behind my right knee, and I sigh at his caress. He trails kisses up my thigh until he reaches my underwear and I squirm, gripping his hair at the feel of his hot breath fanning over me.

"Tsk tsk tsk. That won't do," he says, gazing up at me, before looking around the room. Slowly, he stands with a smirk on his face as he walks over to the wall on other side of the room, taking some of the tinsel down.

"Put your arms up, Claudia," he demands.

A wicked grin spreads across my face as I put my arms above my head, knowing exactly what he's about to do. He grabs a hold of my wrists in one hand and places them up against the wooden post, then wraps the tinsel around them twice, tying them into a tight knot that I can't escape from. My back is arched, and my breathing is heavy as he kneels down in front of me once again.

"Now, where was I?" he asks, biting the inside of my thigh, causing me to squeal.

"Stop being a tease, Henry," I whine.

"As you command."

He winks up at me and rips through my underwear with his bare hands. I gasp and then moan because his mouth is instantly on me, licking and sucking like a man starved. I pull on my restraints, the tinsel digging into my skin as he devours me. My legs involuntarily squeeze together as he has his way with me, but in an instant his hands are there, spreading me and holding me open. I am completely at his mercy.

"Fuck, Henry," I moan.

"Keep moaning my name, sweetheart. I want to feel you come on my tongue."

He inserts two fingers into me with no resistance, and I am dripping for him. He curls them inside of me and the sound that comes out of my mouth is barely human. On and on, he continues with a punishing rhythm until I start to feel my climax building.

"That's it, Claudia. I can feel you squeezing around my fingers. Come for me."

He sucks hard on my clit, and suddenly I'm spiralling over the edge. My back arches and I scream his name as my orgasm takes over all of my senses. He licks me through it, sending spasms through my whole body.

"That's my girl."

"Henry," I whimper.

"What do you need? Tell me."

"I need you to fuck me. Right now," I demand.

He chuckles. "So needy."

Kissing my pussy once more, he stands and kisses me deeply. I can taste myself on his tongue, which only sends me spiralling even further. He quickly unzips his jeans and pulls them down, revealing himself to me. He grasps my hips and lines himself up with my entrance. I can feel the tip of his cock and I press forward to take him, but he pulls back, slightly out of reach.

"Henry," I growl, pulling once again at my restraints.

"Is this what you want?" He presses his tip against me again and I whimper.

"Yes."

"Then it's yours."

He slides himself inside of me, agonisingly slow. I gasp as he buries himself to the hilt, and he kisses me as he starts to pump in and out, building up momentum until he's slamming into me. Screaming his name over and over, he smothers my moans with his mouth, kissing me again as he takes me deeper and deeper.

"Fuck, you feel so good," he hums. "Look at how well you take me." We both look down, watching him pull out and then slide back into me. "Your body was made for me."

I moan again as he picks up his pace. Grasping my hip with one hand to keep me steady, he reaches between us with the other and rubs slow circles on my clit.

"Oh fuck! Yes. Don't stop," I scream, feeling myself get closer and closer to another orgasm.

"Claudia…" Henry moans my name, the sound of it on his lips is my undoing.

"Fuck, Henry. I'm gonna… I'm… *ah!*" My second orgasm crashes over me, blurring my vision. My whole body convulses as Henry continues to pound into me.

"Claudia, fuck…" Henry gasps as he comes, filling me up and gripping my hips so tightly I'm sure it'll leave bruises.

He reaches up and unties my wrists. The tinsel has left tiny marks on my skin and my arms are tender from being held up for so long. I wrap them around his neck and pull him close to me, resting my forehead on his. We're both panting, the world slowly coming back into focus.

I take a deep breath. "That was… woah."

"Yeah. I know," he sighs.

He kisses me tenderly, and my body shivers with a small aftershock.

"I love you," he whispers against my lips.

"I love you more," I reply.

He pulls out of me gently and gets some paper towel, runs it under the tap to make it damp and proceeds to help clean me up. We both get dressed, and I'm now far too hot for all of my layers, to which Henry rolls his eyes and laughs. We're suddenly interrupted by the ringing of the timer.

"Oh yeah… cupcakes and cookies." I giggle.

"We should probably get these cooled and iced if we're to make it to dinner on time."

"Probably."

We pull the cupcakes and cookies out of the oven to cool and clean up the kitchen. There is flour everywhere, and despite our best efforts with the bakery cleanup, we are covered head to toe.

We ice the cupcakes and try one of each for quality control. They're both delicious, and we finish just in time to race home and shower before dinner.

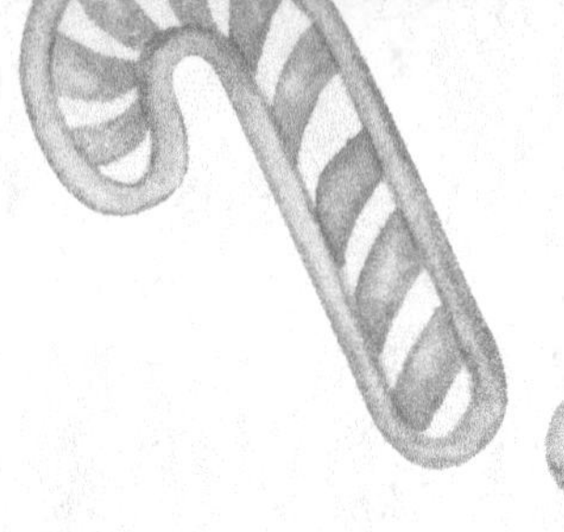

FIFTEEN
Hip Hip Hooray

Henry and I arrive at the restaurant right on 6pm. We haven't seen Lori all day, as she was out celebrating before we even woke up this morning. She's been here for about an hour already, having a couple drinks with her friends before the rest of the family arrive. We place her gift on the table and greet the others, who are all looking very cheery and flushed in the way that only wine can make you appear.

"Happy birthday, Lori." I embrace her and kiss her on the cheek.

"Thank you, darling girl. Hello, my beautiful son!" She grabs Henry and we are suddenly in a three-way hug. Walter catches my eye and we both laugh.

"How many wines have you had already, Mum?" he asks as he escapes.

"Oh, only a bottle. Not much really. Is that for me?" She points to the large gift box on the table.

"It sure is. Happy birthday," he tells her.

She squeaks and claps her hands excitedly, rushing to open her gift. Walter stands by her side with a look of pure adoration for his wife. Her joy is infectious, and we take our seat at the table to watch her open it. She rips off the wrapping paper in one go and promptly lifts the lid, throwing it behind her dramatically. I've decided that I love drunk Lori.

She gasps when she sees what is inside. "What is all of this?" she asks us, pulling out items from the box.

"It's what my family call a goodie box. We tend to make up a box of someone's favourite things for a birthday or Christmas. And we thought you might appreciate a few tastes of Australia. It's an assortment of our favourite things."

Inside the box are two bottles of wine, one from the Barossa Valley and one from McLaren Vale. There are a few different bags of Haighs chocolates, some Fruchocs and Violet Crumbles. We added a jar of Vegemite, a packet of Iced VoVos and Tim Tams. I also included a few jars of goodies from Beerenberg. There's a stuffed koala, a painting that I had commissioned from a local Indigenous artist, some opal earrings, and lastly, a small photo album documenting Henry's time in Australia so far.

"Oh. You two..." Lori trails off. She has tears streaming down her face as she admires each and every item. "This is the most wonderful birthday present. Thank you both." She grabs us both for another hug, and we squeeze her tight as she cries gently into Henry's shirt.

"Are you okay, Mum?" Henry asks.

"Yes, yes." She sniffs. "It's just very thoughtful."

"Vegemite! I haven't had that in years," Walter exclaims.

"That wine looks like a nice drop, Lori," one of her friends pipes up.

"It's one of our favourites," I tell her. "We picked up a case when I took Henry on a wine tour. It was our third date, I believe?"

"Sure was. I saw my first kangaroo on that date," he says proudly.

"Yes you did. And then you cried when you saw a dead one on the side of the road as we drove home and you couldn't understand why I wasn't upset by it."

The whole table erupts with laughter and Henry glares at me.

"Ah son, I should have warned you about the roadkill," Walter says, wiping a tear from his eye.

"It was the wine," he mumbles. "Anyway, should we order some dinner? I'm famished."

I read over the menu again despite having already looked it up online, and decide to order the steak frites.

"I know it's really just steak and chips, but it sounds fancy," I say to the table, and they laugh at me. Henry just shakes his head with a smile on his face. The waitress comes around to take our order.

"Steak frites please. And for the drink can I please have the Pumpkin White Russian cocktail. Thanks," I tell her, and she turns to Henry to take his order.

"Well goodness me, if it isn't Henry Cambell back from Down Under!" she says, grinning at Henry.

"Megan? I didn't even recognise you. How are you?" Henry gets up to give her a hug.

"Good, good. Had a baby since you left, number two on the way," she tells him, rubbing her small baby bump. "I didn't know you were back in town. Josh didn't tell me."

Josh was Henry's best friend growing up. He told me about him as we toured the town a few days after we'd landed. They drifted a little bit after school finished – Henry got swept up in the family business and Josh travelled all over the world before coming back to settle down. He married Megan, his old high school sweetheart, a few months before Henry left. They're still good friends, but their lives are so different now, and the friendship is different.

"I haven't really told anyone else yet that I'm here. Wanted to give us a week or so to settle in and beat the jetlag before we're bombarded with visitors," he says sheepishly.

"Oh okay. No problem, maybe reach out to him soon, yeah? I know he'd love to see you." She turns to me. "And this must be the famous Claudia? Lori here has been telling everyone about you since the minute Henry told her you were together." She smiles at me and I grin back.

"That's me. Only good things, I hope."

"Of course only good things. You're perfect," Lori chimes in, and we all laugh again.

"Well, it was great to finally meet you. Let me take Henry's order and then I'll get that cocktail sorted for you."

Henry orders the rack of lamb with blueberry red wine and a Smoky Old-Fashioned cocktail. I just know that I will be trying some of his meal.

"She seems lovely," I say to Henry.

"Yeah, Megan's great. Her family own this restaurant and she's worked here for years. I didn't know they were expecting baby number two." He frowns slightly.

"You're currently on separate continents. Friendships change. You haven't told him you're here, so I'd say that's tit for tat."

"Yeah, that's true. I'll give him a call tomorrow and organise to catch up for a beer or something."

"Great idea."

After a few minutes, our drinks arrive. I eye my cocktail suspiciously. I wanted to try something uniquely Canadian, and a pumpkin flavoured something sounded about right. It contains vodka, coffee liqueur, pumpkin spice syrup and pumpkin cream. I bring the glass to my mouth and take a sip, closing my eyes to truly savour the taste.

"Well, what do you think?" Henry asks.

"Its… pumpkin-y."

He chuckles.

"It's not bad, it's very different. This is my first pumpkin spice experience."

"I forget that it's not really a thing over in Australia," he says.

"Definitely not a thing, in Adelaide at least. We don't even have a Starbucks there."

"What?" Lori gasps. "No Starbucks?"

"Nope. We have a few chain cafés but most coffee shops are independently owned."

"It's not a bad thing though, really," Henry adds. "I don't drink coffee, but I was almost willing to convert. Adelaide has the best coffee I've ever tasted."

"We do make good coffee," I say proudly, before remembering it's going to be another month before I get to have one again.

Our dinner arrives and we dig in. The steak is cooked perfectly and the chips are crunchy, with the perfect amount of salt. The conversation at the table is flowing, and Lori's friends are having a blast picking on my accent and asking every ridiculous question about Australia you can think of. When Megan comes to clear the last of the plates, Henry whispers in her ear that we're ready for the cupcakes and asks if he can duck into the kitchen to bring them out.

Suddenly, the lights are dimmed and in walks Henry with a tray full of red velvet cupcakes adorned with candles.

Happy birthday to you
Happy birthday to you
Happy birthday, dear Lori!
Happy birthday to you!

"Hip hip…"

Silence.

Everyone looks at me confused. I'm confused. Henry is shaking with laughter.

"Hip hip?" Megan asks.

"Ah… is that not a thing here?"

They look at me blankly.

"You know, hip hip, hooray! Hip hip, hooray! Hip hip, hooray!"

"Sorry sweetheart, I should have warned you. That's definitely an Aussie thing." Henry chuckles, as the others start to laugh.

"Well, that's embarrassing. Karma for telling everyone the kangaroo story, I guess. Anyway… shall we eat the cupcakes? Henry and I baked these fresh this morning." My face is as pink as the icing. The cakes are shared around the table, and I try to hide my mortification. One of Lori's friends demands to know more about the Australian birthday song tradition, and Megan places another cocktail down in front of me.

"On the house." She winks as she walks away.

We spend the rest of the evening comparing the differences of our countries, from language to food to traditions. Eventually, the night wraps up and we start to say our goodbyes, with promises to spend time together again before we go back to Australia.

As the four of us – Walter, Henry, Lori and I – get into a taxi, Lori's friends start singing 'hip hip, hooray' and almost fall over each other laughing.

I'm feeling warm and giddy from the cocktails, and full of love from the company, my embarrassment mostly forgotten.

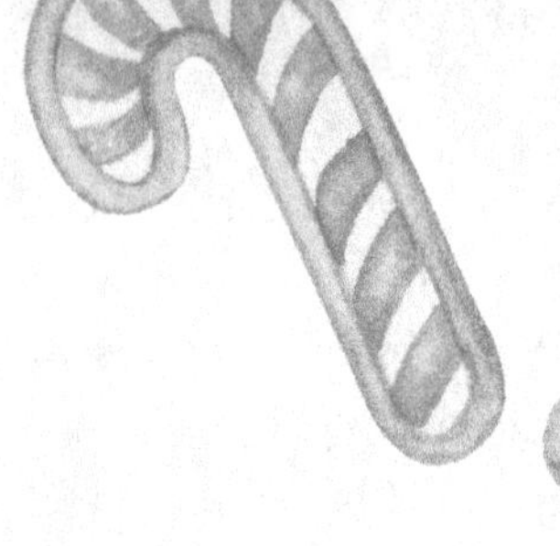

SIXTEEN
Fireworks

Tonight is the Light Up the Night festival, signifying the start of the Christmas season. The sun has set, and as we walk into the main part of town, the streets come alive. The spirit of Christmas is well and truly in the air, now that December has hit. The snow is finally sticking to the ground, much to my delight, and piles of fluffy snow line the footpaths around the town centre. In the middle of the town, the Grand Falls on the Mississippi are slick with ice, the river starting to freeze over in some places. The temperature tonight is minus three degrees, and I am wearing as many layers as possible to the festival, as most of it is outside.

Every street light is wrapped in Christmas lights or tinsel. Christmas carols play softly over the speakers. Shop fronts are decorated in ribbons, baubles and garlands, twinkling lights hang from every surface, and every building has at least one Christmas tree decorating their doorway. The smell of pine and cinnamon and roasted chestnuts permeates the air, and the joyous laughter of children fills my ears.

Market stalls line the streets, with vendors selling local wares ranging from baked goods, homemade toys and clothing, old books and art. We peruse the streets for a while, stopping at every stall. Henry knows everyone, and my cheeks are already hurting from meeting so many new people and smiling. It's a good type of pain, though. Because for the first time, I feel as though I can have the Christmas I always wanted. There is magic in the air here, and I fear I may be falling in love.

We pick up dinner from one of the food vans, and I finally get a taste of a traditional poutine. We have chips, cheese and gravy back home but this was something else entirely. Perfectly cooked chips, hot salty gravy combined with creamy cheese curds – I don't think I've eaten anything so fast in my life.

"Time for some hot cocoa, and a little Almonte tradition," Henry tells me as we stop by one of the cafés.

"Sounds good to me."

We get to the counter, and of course Henry knows the older man working and has a quick catch up, introducing me and giving him a brief wrap up of his time abroad.

"Anyway, can I please have two large hot cocoas with Vodkow."

"Vodkow?"

"Trust me, you're going to love it," he tells me.

"Okay but what is it?"

"It's a locally produced spirit, distilled from milk. It's creamy and has a hint of vanilla. The perfect addition to a hot cocoa."

"That sounds so good!"

The man hands us over our drinks and I take a tentative sip, moaning in delight at the taste.

"Oh my god, this is the best hot chocolate I've ever had in my entire life," I say, taking another big sip and almost scalding my tongue.

"Good, eh?" Henry replies.

"So good. How many can we have?"

He kisses the top of my head. "As many as you want."

We walk hand-in-hand around the streets, popping in and out of shops. Henry gives me a more in-depth run down of the town history. Apparently the inventor of basketball was from Almonte and there's a statue of him in the centre of town. We bump into Megan and Josh, who Henry finally told we were here, and have a drink with some of his old school friends. It's super fun watching him interact with people he has known his whole life. He seems more relaxed here, like he doesn't have to try as hard. He feels at home, and I start to wonder once again about our future, except this time, I picture myself living here instead.

The thought takes me by surprise, as I've never even considered leaving Australia. But the more I think about it, and the more time I spend here, it feels like a choice I'd be willing to make. I love my job and my friends and my family, but realistically there isn't anything tying me down. Henry has his family legacy to continue, and I could never force him to choose between his lifelong dream and me.

Oh boy, I need another Vodkow, I think to myself. And to have a conversation with Henry.

"Claudia, you with us?"

I blink, shaken out of my spiralling thoughts by Henry's deep tone.

"Huh?"

"I said, Santa is almost here if you want to go and have a look."

"Oh, yeah of course. I love Santa."

"I think you're going to really love this Santa." He winks.

We walk to the main stage at the end of the street, the carol singers have taken a momentary pause and a woman dressed in an elf suit is talking into the microphone.

"Okay folks, get those kids of yours lined up and ready because Santa is on his way. What I need to hear from you is one big loud, *Ho, Ho, Ho!* Can you do that for me? In three, two one…"

"Ho, Ho, Ho!" the crowd shouts, the children screaming at the top of their lungs.

"I think we can do better than that. One more time, are you ready? Three, two one…"

"HO, HO, HO!" we all scream, and onto the stage walks Santa and Mrs Claus, who look a little too familiar.

"No way," I breathe.

Henry smiles proudly. "Yep."

Lori and Walter wave at us from the stage, Walter giving me a wink before he sits on Santa's chair. The elf passes the microphone to him, and he clears his throat loudly.

"Ho, Ho, Ho, Merry Christmas, everyone! Have you all been good this year?" he asks the crowd, to which the children respond with a resounding yes.

"Wonderful. I can't wait to meet you all in just a moment. But first, I want to invite a very special guest onto the stage. She's visiting us all the way from Australia, which is even further away from here than the North Pole, and this is her very first Almonte Christmas. Claudia, will you please join me up here?" He points a white gloved finger at me, and everyone turns to look my way.

My face turns bright red as the crowd parts, allowing me a clear path to the stage. I look at Henry, who is smothering a laugh, his eyes crinkling at the sides when he takes in my expression.

"Oh you are so dead," I force out through my teeth as I plaster on a smile.

The crowd starts to chant my name and I have no choice but to make my way up to the stage to sit with Santa. Walter pats the arm of the chair for me to sit on, and I roll my eyes but sit down because all eyes are on me.

I lean in to whisper in Walter's ear, "Did your son put you up to this?"

"I decline to answer that question," he whispers back. Turning to face the crowd once more, he picks up the microphone.

"So dear Claudia, how are you liking Almonte so far?"

He holds out the microphone to me and I lean in. "I think it's the most magical place I've ever been to. Everyone has been so kind, I already feel like I'm at home here."

I make eye contact with Henry in the crowd as I say this, and I see his lips part with a soft exhale.

"That's lovely. And is Christmas your favourite time of the year? It sure is mine!" he chortles, and the crowd laughs.

I swallow hard and decide to give a somewhat honest answer.

"Christmas is… a hard time for me. I'll admit, it has been a long time since I've felt the joy and magic of Christmas. But being here… being here is definitely changing my perspective. There's just something about this place, it's almost dreamlike. Like out of a Hallmark movie."

That elicits a laugh out of the crowd, and the smile on my face is genuine and true.

"Well, all of us here are lucky to have you for Christmas and we hope to make it as magical as possible. Thank you for being here, Claudia."

"Thank you for having me, Santa."

I stand from the chair and the crowd applauds. I give Santa – Walter – a hug and turn to embrace Lori.

"You'll always have a home here. I hope you know that," she whispers into my ear.

The statement and the meaning behind it brings tears to my eyes.

"Thank you, Lori." I squeeze her tight and then walk off stage, back into Henry's awaiting arms.

He notices the tears in my eyes but doesn't say anything, just kisses me softly and holds me tight. He knows how much this means to me. The children all line up for a visit with Santa and we treat ourselves to another Vodkow hot cocoa.

"Come," Henry says as he takes my hand. "We need to get the best spot for the fireworks."

"You didn't mention fireworks!" I gasp.

"Surprise." He chuckles.

I love fireworks. I love the colours and the sounds and the patterns. They always bring me so much joy. It probably has something to do with healing my inner child. My parents used to take Gabi and I to a fireworks show every Christmas, but as with every other tradition, that stopped when they got divorced.

We walk towards the bridge that crosses over the Mississippi Falls, beelining for the perfect viewing point. The crowds have started forming, toddlers sleeping in their prams and children sitting on their parents' shoulders. A few kids are having a snowball fight and building snow men, and I smile at their unfiltered joy.

Speakers have been set up along the street, "Underneath the Tree" by Kelly Clarkson setting the mood. Christmas lights shimmer from the trees and the rooftops, casting a soft glow over the gathering crowd. Much to my delight, snow starts falling in a light sprinkle. I am giddy with joy, and Vodkow, and stick out my tongue in the hopes to catch a snowflake.

"Having fun?" Henry smirks.

"I hate to admit it, but yes," I tell him.

Santa and Mrs Claus reappear on the bridge to lead us all in a countdown for the fireworks. Henry stands behind me and wraps his arms around my waist.

"Get ready," Henry murmurs.

"Ten, nine, eight…"

"This reminds me of our first kiss at New Year's," I say, looking up at him with a grin.

"Seven, six…"

"It does. Claudia?"

"Five, four…"

"Yes?" I giggle.

"Three…"

"Can I kiss you?"

"Two, one…"

"Please," I breathe, and he dazzles me with a smile that sends my knees weak.

"Merry Christmas!"

Henry kisses me tenderly as the fireworks launch into the air with a whistle. The first of them crack open the sky, exploding in shades of red and gold. Gasps ripple through the crowd and cheers of joy ring through the air as golden lights trail across the sky, looking like falling stars. More are launched into the air, exploding into snowflake-like shapes, others crackling into icy shades of silver and blue. The show is synchronised with the Christmas classic, "It's the Most Wonderful Time of the Year" by Andy Williams, everyone is singing along, some are dancing in the street. Nothing could wipe the smile off of my face, not even the tears threatening to spill over at the feeling of pure joy and nostalgia that's washing over me.

As the song reaches its crescendo, the pace of the fireworks quicken. A burst of red, green, pink and blue, every colour imaginable booms and crackles across the sky. As the music reaches its peak, the sky is so full of light and colour it's as bright as if it were the middle of the day. Tears are streaming down my face now as Henry holds me tight, kissing them away. He doesn't say anything, he doesn't need to, because he knows that these are happy and joyous tears. Healing tears.

The last of the fireworks fizzle out into silence, and the crowd erupts in applause. Everyone's faces are lit with wonder, and I've never felt a more collective feeling of togetherness in a community than I do at this very moment. The spirit of Christmas has awoken within me, and my inner child is feeling at peace.

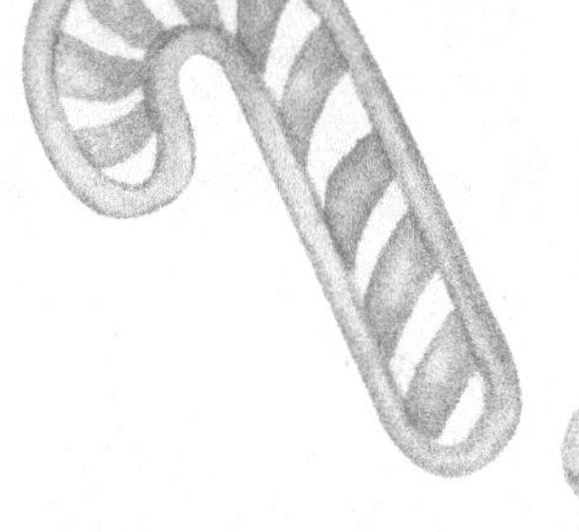

SEVENTEEN
Christmas Tree Farm

"I am so excited!" I squeal from the passenger seat of the car.

"Well, I didn't think I'd hear those words come out of your mouth about anything Christmas related. It's a Christmas miracle!" Henry sings.

"Oh ha-ha. Don't get too excited just yet. Anything can happen between now and Christmas day to ruin things."

"That's such a scrooge way of thinking."

"I'm a realist. And the reality is I haven't enjoyed Christmas in years. So if I want to bah humbug, I'm gonna bah humbug."

He rolls his eyes at me but a small smile plays on his lips. "Not today though?" he asks.

"Not today. We are about to cut our own Christmas tree, at a real Christmas tree farm, in the snow. I feel like I'm in a movie."

"Isn't there a Christmas tree farm in Adelaide somewhere?"

"There is, but cutting down a tree in forty-degree heat, sur-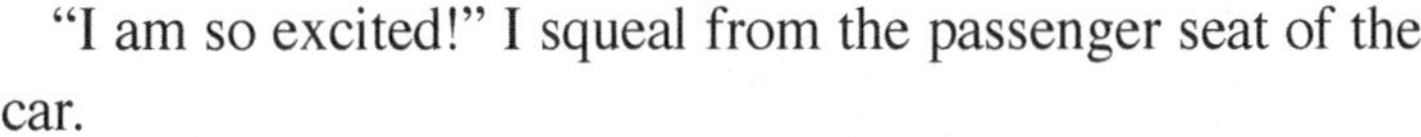rounded by signs saying, *'watch for snakes!'* and having the damn tree all but die by Christmas day… isn't really festive."

He laughs. "Okay, you got me. That doesn't sound very Christmas-y. At least it seems that I've picked the absolute best day for us to get our tree."

It is the most picturesque winter's day I have ever seen. It snowed all day yesterday and all night, and there's at least twenty centimetres of fresh snow on the ground. White, fluffy clouds dapple the pale blue sky, allowing the sunshine to peek through. It's still bitterly cold, but it's not windy or raining or snowing. The weather is absolutely perfect, and I can't wait to explore this farm.

"It really is beautiful. I imagine it's just as stunning during summer as well." I sigh.

"It is. And there's so much to do around here during the summer. We'll have to come back and I'll show you. We can go canoeing on the river, go on a bike ride along the Ottawa Valley Rail Trail, or I could take you down to Lanark County. There's so many hikes and trails and lakes…"

Henry continues talking animatedly about all of the things we could do together when we visit next. I let him talk, and contribute when I can, but in my head I'm spiralling. Everything he's telling me sounds like a dream. I can see myself packing up my life and moving here so easily, and it's terrifying. Almonte has everything I need. And Henry… Henry has his family and his business. His legacy. He can't leave all of this behind. For me? No way.

Before coming here, I was so scared of him coming home and not wanting to go back to Australia. But now that we've been here almost a month, I'm not worried about him leaving me. I'm worried that I might push him too fast when I suggest that I could be willing to move here for *him*. We live together, and he's been very forthcoming with what he wants out of life, but we've never discussed the possibility of me moving. I know I've been too scared of what he'll say. And he has probably been too scared to tell me that he can't stay in Australia. But something strange has happened, and I'm suddenly contemplating uprooting my life…

"Claudia?"

"Hmm? Yep?"

"Daydreaming, are we?" Henry laughs.

"A little. Did you say something?" I ask, trying to not let on that I've just been freaking out internally.

"I said we're almost here."

It's only a short drive from Henry's house to the farm. We turn off the main road and onto a smaller street, a Cedar Hill Christmas Tree Farm sign guiding the way. We borrowed Walter's car for the day and it's big enough to easily strap a Christmas tree to the roof. We turn down another dirt road, and my excitement levels peak as hundreds of Christmas trees come into view. Some are only a few feet tall, while others stand proudly at well over twelve feet.

The trees, now blanketed in white from last night's snowfall, glisten in the morning sun. Their branches are heavy with the soft powder. Each one looks like it's been dipped in icing sugar, standing in neat rows, stretching out further than I can see them, and a sign welcomes us to the farm as we pull into the driveway.

"This is going to be a great day. I just know it," I say to Henry.

"Just you wait and see."

We park the car and climb out, donning our extra thick winter coats as we do. Someone has been through and ploughed the main drive and walkway, and the red barn-style farm shop comes into view as we walk along the path, gravel and snow crunching beneath our boots. The shop is trimmed in evergreen garlands and classic white string lights. Smoke curls up lazily from a chimney, and the smell of pine and cinnamon fills my nose.

We decided to come during the week so it wasn't as busy, and there aren't too many other people around, which is surprising to me. Christmas is only a week away. The fact that so many people only buy their trees a week out from Christmas is mind blowing. When I was putting up my tree, it was always on the day of the Adelaide Christmas Pageant. It was tradition. And that normally occurred around mid to late November, so our trees were normally up for at least a month, if not longer. But I guess my tree was plastic, so I imagine a real one is a bit harder to look after than my cheap plastic one at home.

"Hello, folks. How can we help you two today?" says a man wearing a thick jumper with the farm logo embroidered on the chest pocket.

"Carl! You're still here?" Henry says joyfully, reaching out to shake the old man's hand.

"Well, I'll be damned. Henry Cambell, back from Australia. I thought you were supposed to be gone for a while yet."

"Just visiting home for the holidays. We go back just a few days into the new year. Carl, this is Claudia. Claudia, this is Carl."

"Hi Claudia, you're even more lovely than Lori said," Carl says, taking my hand in his for a handshake. His grip is firm but friendly.

I blush. "Thank you. God, has Lori told the whole town about me?"

They both chuckle.

"Carl has worked here since before I was even a thought in my mum's mind."

"Way to make a man feel old, Henry."

"You are old," Henry teases.

Carl harrumphs and glares daggers at Henry, before the two of them break out into laughter and give each other a big hug.

"It's good to see you back, Henry. I know your mum's been missing you. Your dad too. Hell, we all have. No one can make croissants like you," Carl tells him, and I smile at the compliment. He's not wrong.

"I've missed them too. I've missed everyone. But I'm having a great time in Australia. I'm doing everything I wanted to do.

I'll come home if and when I'm ready." He smiles, almost sadly. "I even found love over there, something I never thought would happen. And yet here she is."

He wraps an arm around my waist and pulls me in tight to his side. Looking up at him, I smile. It never gets old listening to Henry just openly telling anyone and everyone how much he loves me.

"Aw. That's beautiful."

"We're here to get a tree. Any chance you could drop us off so we can cut one ourselves? Claudia has never cut a Christmas tree before," Henry tells Carl.

"Of course I can. It'll be my honour to be a part of your first Christmas tree farm experience. Shall we take the tractor wagon? I'll make sure no one else gets on so you can have it to yourselves."

"That would be great, thanks Carl."

We make our way over to one of the tractor led wagons, it's bright red and big enough to carry passengers and their Christmas trees. As I climb into it, I feel as though I'm stepping into Santa's sleigh. We each find a blanket to drape over our knees, as Carl starts the engine, preparing to take us to our stop on the farm.

"Okay. So we have a big decision to make..." Henry trails off.

I swiftly turn my head to look at him, shocked, because I don't think this is really the time or place to be having a serious discussion.

"We do... but do you really want to talk about it now, though?"

"Well yeah. I don't think we have a choice."

I take a deep breath in and let it out slowly before replying. "Okay. What are you thinking?"

He ponders for a moment. "Well, we have quite a few options. We have the traditional Fraser Fir with soft needles, holds ornaments well, smells like Christmas. There's the Balsam Fir, which always smells amazing. It has softer branches and is more old-school. The Koreana Fir is smaller but super pretty, and it almost looks frosted. Then there's Scotch Pine, Blue Spruce, White Spruce…"

I stare at him blankly for a moment, blinking.

"Ohhhh. You're talking about which tree we should get." I laugh. *Of course* it's about our choice of Christmas tree.

"Well, yeah. What else would it be about?" he asks, tilting his head.

"Nothing! Don't worry about it. So, trees. What type of tree do you normally get?"

"We normally go for a Fraser Fir, but I also like to wander around and find the one that speaks to me the most. This year, you have the honour of choosing the tree."

"Me?"

"Yes, you. You are our guest of honour. And also the love of my life who I am trying to convince that Christmas is the most magical time of year. Of course you get to choose the tree."

"No pressure or anything," I laugh nervously.

"Finding the perfect Christmas tree is like finding the perfect girlfriend. When you know, you know," he says, amused.

"Did you just compare me to a tree?"

"Well, you are perfect, so…"

I elbow him in his side, which he laughs off and then proceeds to wrap his arm around my shoulder, pulling me in close. Tilting my chin up with his finger, he kisses me softly. The warmth of his lips is a nice contrast in comparison to the chill. I may brush off his comments, but his words bury themselves deep within me and I fall for him even further than I thought I could.

We slowly drive around the farm, crossing over the infamous covered bridge, which I was told has featured in many Hallmark movies. We quickly hop out of the tractor for a cute photo op-portunity. The bridge is decorated in garlands of gold and red, and the roof is packed with fresh snow. It looks like something from a postcard. Carl is quite the photographer, and we flick through the one hundred or so photos he snapped as we ride in the back of the tractor, making our way to our destination.

After a few short minutes, we pull up next to a field with rows and rows of Christmas trees, all of varying sizes and shades of green. Some are a deep forest green, the kind of green you immediately associate with Christmas. Others are a soft sage green or a silvery green-grey.

"I have no idea how I'm supposed to choose a tree," I whine.

"You don't choose the tree. The tree chooses you. Let's just wander around for a while. It's a beautiful day and we have absolutely nothing else planned."

"You are weirdly passionate about Christmas trees," I say.

"It's serious business," he says proudly, slightly puffing out his chest.

I laugh and take his hand in mine as we begin our hunt. The snow crunches softly beneath our boots, and our breath clouds the air, but the sun is shining and the company is wonderful. We make small conversation, as my mind continues to whirl about conversations we are yet to have.

"This really is perfect," I tell him.

He squeezes my hand. "It's one of my favourite places to visit. They open up for the fall too – they have a pumpkin patch and the kids come out and play and go on tractor rides. It's so much fun."

"I wish we celebrated fall, or autumn, as you guys do. We have Easter in autumn, but it's just not the right vibe. Halloween on a hot day just doesn't make sense."

"I agree. It felt so odd when we went to that party last year and all of my face paint was sweating off."

"Yeah," I laugh. "You looked like a half-melted Dracula by the end of the night."

We fall into an easy silence, and I busy myself by looking around at the different trees. Nothing has jumped out at me yet, they all look the same to me, like a Christmas tree.

Henry clears his throat. "So, the other night. You said you already feel like you're at home here. Did you mean that?"

I slow our pace as I think about what I'm going to say next.

"I did. I do. This place makes me feel… at peace, I guess. Like there's no pressure on me to do anything or be anyone, you know?"

"I know. It's the best part about Almonte."

He pauses, and we stop walking altogether. I turn to look at him, and he has a contemplative look on his face.

"I think we've been avoiding the topic of our cross-continental relationship. But we really should talk about what our future looks like."

I swallow the lump forming in my throat. "You're right. We have. I'll be honest, I'm scared. I have been since the moment we decided to give us a go."

"I know. I am too. I have an idea of what I want, but I want to know where your head is. What are you thinking?"

"I don't want to push you too much…" I trail off. Do I just come right out and say what I've been contemplating?

"You won't." He takes both of my hands in his. "I love you, Claudia. Whatever we decide to do, it will be a joint decision."

He rubs his thumb over my knuckles, and the motion calms me, though my heart is still racing.

"Okay." I pause and take in a breath. "Over the last few weeks, I've been seriously thinking about where I am in life and how happy I am in my current circumstances."

He says nothing but nods encouragingly.

"And being here has given me some room to breathe and to think. And I think I know what I want to do."

"And what is that?" he asks gently.

"I want to live a slow and easy life. I want to go for quiet walks in the mornings and have bakery treats whenever I want them. I want to be surrounded by nature. I want to be with you."

He pulls me in closer and wraps his arms around my waist. "So what are you saying?"

"I know how much you love this town. I know how much you love the bakery and want to continue the family legacy. I could never, ever ask you to give that up for me. So... so what I'm saying is that I can see myself relocating here with you, whenever you're ready to come back home. I want to live this life with you, Henry."

An errant tear slides down my cheek and he catches it with his thumb.

"You would uproot your life and move here, for me?"

"Not *for* you. *With* you. And for myself, I think. Sure, I have friends and family back home, and I have a career in teaching, but really I have nothing holding me there. I want to live a life without the noise and pressure."

Henry's smile could light up a thousand dark rooms. His eyes dance, and I realise now they are swimming with tears.

Grabbing my face with both hands, he kisses me deeply, his tears mingling with mine.

"I have never met a more selfless, beautiful, incredible woman in my entire life. How did I get so lucky to be able to call you mine?"

I laugh against his lips.

"Are you sure, sweetheart? We can think it over, there's no rush."

"I'm about... ninety percent sure. Obviously I still need to look into the logistics, what I would do for work and all of that. Plus, I am positive I will have a freak out moment about it at some stage and focus on everything that could go wrong. But now that I've said it out loud, I know I want this."

He kisses me again, and it's a kiss with the promise of forever.

"I love you, Claudia."

"I love you too," I whisper.

"For what it's worth, I would move for you if you asked me to."

"I know," I tell him. "I was actually worried you wouldn't want me to relocate. I didn't want to come off too strong." I laugh, thinking how ridiculous it is that I even thought that way.

He gives me a deadpan look.

"Too strong? We've been together for almost two years. We live together. We've talked about marriage and kids..."

"Okay, you got me there. Call me anxious, I guess."

"Understandable. If you ever feel that way again, just talk to me. I will always listen."

"Thank you."

As we stand there, tears drying on our cheeks and hearts full, I look around at the trees surrounding us. The one to my left catches my eye, and I walk over to it to run my hand along its branches. Its needles are soft to the touch and are a beautiful blue-green shade. It stands at about seven feet, and the branches are dense. It looks like all of the others, but for some reason, I'm drawn to it.

"I think this is the one," I tell Henry.

"A Fraser Fir. Excellent choice."

"I think it heard us make a big life decision and wanted to be a part of our story." I laugh.

"Like I said, the tree chooses you. Let's get hacking."

Henry had bought a hand saw from home to cut the tree down. Taking off his coat, he rolls up his sleeves to reveal thick forearms, perfect for tree cutting. I step back and watch him at work, because I am just like every other girl, and watching my man chop down a tree does something to me.

"That is insanely hot, babe."

"Hmm?" Henry says, wiping the sweat from his brow. I nearly pass away.

"I would like you to be naked the moment we get home," I tell him, still struggling to remain upright.

He throws his head back and laughs. "You are such a perv."

"I won't even try to deny it." I grin.

He cuts through the bough of the tree and it comes crashing

down onto the snow. At that moment, Carl comes back around the corner on the tractor, ready to heave it back to the farm shop to be shaken and wrapped.

I feel giddy as we sit in the back of the tractor, my heart pounding from horny adrenaline, but also from declaring that I will move continents for this man. I feel so incredibly happy that I might burst.

We pull up to the farm, and Carl and a few other staff members take our tree away. We decide to warm up by the outdoor fire with some hot apple cider as we wait.

"I've never had hot apple cider before," I admit as Henry hands me a cup.

"It's basically just warmed up apple juice with a few spices, but it's alcoholic."

"Sounds great to me."

I take a whiff of the drink in my hand, detecting notes of apple, cinnamon, clove and maybe a hint of orange. Bringing the steaming cup to my lips, I take a sip and am surprised by how delicious it is.

"Oh wow. It's like a Christmas explosion in my mouth," I say to Henry.

"Well, that's one way to describe it," he laughs.

We continue chatting, mostly about what food we'll be having for Christmas, when suddenly I'm hit in the shoulder by a snowball. I turn in the direction it came from, and another comes at me, knocking my drink from my hands.

"What the hell? Who's throwing that?" I whine.

I look out and can vaguely see someone standing behind a tree.

"You better apologise, whoever you are, you just knocked my drink from my hands!" I yell at the figure.

"Guess I owe you another one," a voice booms.

A voice I recognise all too well.

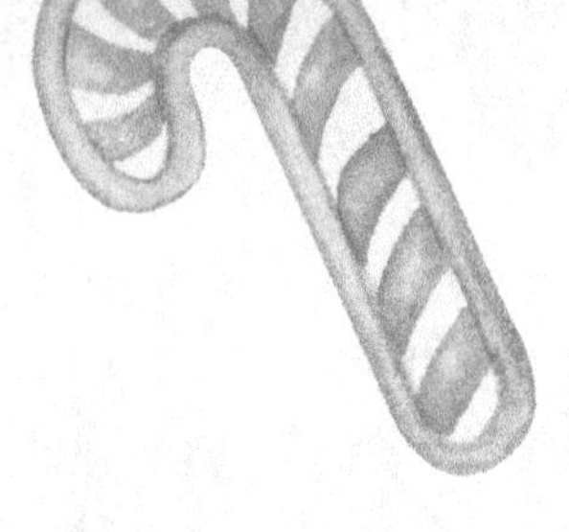

EIGHTEEN
Surprise

"Oh my god!"

"Surprise," Nath says with a mischievous grin.

I run over to my cousin and jump into his arms. His warm and familiar scent washes over me, making me tear up again.

"What? How? When? Huh?" I am lost for words.

"It was all Henry's idea. He said it would be great for you to have a piece of home with you for Christmas, I had the money saved, felt like travelling and thought, why not surprise you."

"Well, consider me absolutely surprised. I can't believe you're here!" I squeal and hug him again.

"Me too, Claud. I've missed you."

"I've missed you too. God, how is the family going to cope without us both at Christmas this year?"

"They have a baby to dote over. They won't even notice us missing."

"True. Oh man, it's going to be so nice not to be insulted this year. You're going to love Henry's family."

"I already do. They picked me up from the airport this morning." He hikes his thumb over his shoulder and Lori and Walter are standing by their car, waving at us.

"Cheeky buggers."

"They love you, Claud. Truly. They would not stop talking about you the entire drive here."

A blush spreads across my cheeks.

"They really are wonderful people," I tell him. "And this place… Nath, I'm in love. This town and the people. It's magical."

"And Christmas? Are you back in love with it yet?" he teases.

"We're getting there. Won't know until it happens."

Henry walks over to where we are standing and gives Nath a hug, lifting him off his feet.

"I forgot how tall you are," Nath grunts as he's dropped back down on the ground.

"I've missed you, my friend," Henry says, and my heart hurts from seeing two of my favourite people in the world getting along so well.

"You too, mate."

"Nath, you owe me a drink," I say, gesturing to my discarded mug lying in the snow. "I say we all have one, and then get this tree loaded up so we can get back home and decorate it."

"Wow. I can't remember the last time you were keen to decorate a tree. In fact," Nath taps his finger against his chin in contemplation, "I can't remember the last time you even had a Christmas tree."

"Henry and I had one last year," I point out.

"No, Henry got one for you last year and you watched him decorate it while grumbling the whole time and acting like the Grinch."

"That's true," Henry chimes in, and I glare at him.

"Okay. Well. Things are changing. God, can't a girl have a little growth?" I roll my eyes, but I know they're toying with me.

"We're just teasing," Nath says. "But in all seriousness, yes, let's get this tree Christma-fied."

***

Once we get back to the house, Lori pours us all a glass of wine and puts on some Christmas carols. The five of us spend the afternoon singing along to the songs completely out of tune, whilst chaotically decorating the tree. There is absolutely no rhyme or reason to how it's decorated. No colour scheme, no evenly spread baubles. Everyone just goes to town on this tree, and now it looks like an explosion of glitter and lights. I love it so much, and I can feel my grouchy heart starting to thaw as the Christmas spirit gently seeps in.

Nath and I are sitting on the front porch steps, a glass of wine in hand, wrapped in coats and a huge blanket covering us, reminiscing about Christmases past.

"I can't remember the last time I truly enjoyed Christmas with our family," I say. It's bitterly cold outside now, and my breath fogs the air when I speak.

"I know. I don't cop it anywhere near as much as you do, probably because I'm a guy, which is stupid." Nath scoffs. "I don't particularly hate Christmas, but I do dread it every year that you're there because I just know they are going to ruin it for you, and it makes me so mad."

"We could never stand up to them though. Could you imagine?"

Nath shudders. "No way. Watching Henry do it last year was like watching a soap opera. I think Mum is still sulking about that."

"Yeah that was both exhilarating and terrifying. I'm surprised they still speak to him after that, though it did take a while for them to look past it."

"Bunch of children," he grumbles.

"They probably think that if they scare him away, I'll never find another boyfriend."

He laughs. "It's sad, but you might be on the money there."

We fall into a comfortable silence and I sip at my wine, looking out over the street. Snow is lightly falling, and the streets are quiet as everyone settles in for the night. There's a soft hum of traffic from the centre of town, but otherwise it's almost silent. I take in a deep breath and then exhale loudly.

"You're different here," Nath says quietly. "You look at ease. Relaxed and carefree."

"I feel different."

He nods his head, lost in his own thoughts.

"Nath, I think I'm going to move here," I all but whisper.

"I know. I could have guessed as soon as I saw you with his family. You looked like you again. The old you, the pre-divorce and shitty ex-boyfriend you. I knew as soon as you walked into this house as if it was home, that you might be making it so."

A single tear slides down my cheek and I hastily wipe it away.

"Is it truly what you want?" he asks gently.

"It is. I can't explain it, but it just feels right. I'm going to miss everyone so much though. It won't be straight away, but I think this is where I want to end up. This feels like what home should be."

Nath leans over and takes my hand, giving it a gentle squeeze. "You know… the family is going to freak the fuck out over this."

I choke out a laugh. "Oh, don't I know it. Please keep it a secret though. I'll tell them when it's the right time."

"Pinky promise, I won't tell a soul." He locks his little finger with mine.

"Thank you…" I pause. "I'm really, really happy."

"Good. It's about damn time, Claud. You deserve it."

NINETEEN
Christmas Eve
2025

"I can't believe you did this," Henry says, shocked.

"I know. I don't know what has come over me."

Standing in our bedroom, looking at ourselves in the full-length mirror, I admire the matching Christmas pyjama set we're wearing. Red tartan pants and top with a cute little reindeer on the front, complete with a glittery, red pompom nose. It's disgustingly adorable, and I have zero regrets buying them after seeing Henry wearing them.

"They're perfectly hideous. I love them." He grins.

"Good." I giggle. *I giggle.* About Christmas pyjamas. What has happened to me?

"When did you buy these?"

"Two days ago, you were off running errands and your mum and I decided to do some last-minute shopping."

"Sneaky."

"I thought I'd better give myself something to laugh about, seeing as we're video calling my family later tonight."

"I'm sure it will be fine. They can't ruin Christmas via a video call. Surely." Henry frowns.

"Not intentionally. But the best part about calling them is if they annoy me or insult me, I can just hang up," I say cheerfully.

"Very true. Plus, I know my mum – you get a few mulled wines into her and she'll have something to say if they start saying anything remotely rude to you."

"Speaking of your mum, do you think we should tell your parents about our plan?"

"We can, but only if you're ready."

"I'll see where the night takes us. Do you think they'll be excited?"

"I think Mum will cry. They're going to be so happy. They really do love you."

"Well, they better, because they're going to get real sick of me otherwise." I laugh.

We make our way downstairs, the smell of mulled wine and gingerbread greeting us. I've been told that we can open some gifts tonight, as a lot of Canadian families open their presents on Christmas Eve. The Cambell family like to do a bit of both.

As we enter the living room, Lori screeches with laughter over our matching ensemble.

"Oh my god. You two look like something out of a movie. I knew they would look ridiculous on you, Henry."

"Hey, I think they look cute," Henry whines.

"Oh yes, son. Very cute," Walter says, walking into the lounge room with his own hideous Christmas jumper on.

"Wow Walter. That is positively awful. I love it," I tease.

"Thank you, Claudia."

He spins around to give us a full view of the jumper. It's adorned in a mix of red, blue and green Christmas icons, like trees and reindeer. It is so mismatched and uncoordinated, it looks like something the sewing machine just spat out.

"Wanna see the best part?" Walter says.

"Absolutely."

He turns around and starts fiddling with a few things, and then in an instant, his jumper lights up in a multitude of colours.

"Ta-da! It has lights!" he says, pointing to his now twinkling jumper.

"That is brilliant. I fear that I may need one," I tell him.

"Maybe I'll get you one for next year." He winks.

"My god, it's like Christmas threw up on all of you," Nath interrupts.

"Like you can talk." Henry points out his shirt that has a picture of Kevin from *Home Alone* on it, with the quote *'Merry Christmas, ya filthy animal'*.

"This is classy," Nath says, waving a hand over his front. "You all look like you stepped out of a cheesy Christmas catalogue. I'm most surprised by you, Claud. You're wearing Christmas apparel. By choice." He narrows his eyes. "Henry, what have you done to her?"

Henry laughs and wraps an arm around my shoulder. "All I did was love her right, and keep the promise I made," he says, and my heart soars.

"Gross." Nath rolls his eyes.

"Lori, come on now, where's your Chrissy shirt? You're the odd one out!" I say.

"Chrissy?" she laughs. "Walt used to call it that way back in the day, right when I first met him."

"I've lost my Australian-ness!" says Walter, and we all laugh.

"I have a jumper. Let me go get it."

She races back upstairs as we all sit at the table and help ourselves to some of the mulled wine steaming in a pot in the middle of the table. The house is awash with a soft glow from the fireplace and the lights on the Christmas tree, creating a festive ambience. Christmas carols play gently from the record player in the lounge, and I let myself sit in the moment to absorb everything.

"Are you okay?" Henry asks.

I nod. "Just taking it all in. I can't remember the last time I spent a Christmas so… calm. There's no stress or anxiety. I'm just here, surrounded by amazing people in a magical Christmas town. I'm content, and it's a nice feeling."

He takes my hand and brushes a kiss over my knuckles, sending a light shiver down my spine. "This is how Christmas should be."

I smile at him, because he's right.

Lori's footsteps sound on the stairs and we all look up in time to see her posing with her Christmas jumper. We all laugh, and then I gasp. Her jumper is pink and green, adorned in Christmas patterns, but stitched on the front of it is a list of names. Lori, Walter, Henry… and Claudia.

"Lori…" I choke out.

"I had it made especially this year. What do you think?" she says proudly.

I don't think. I get up from the table and wrap my arms around the woman who has made me feel like this place could be my home. She squeezes me tight as she leans in to whisper in my ear, "You're part of the family now, Claudia."

Tears line my eyes as I manage a reply. "I love it," is all I can get out.

We break apart and she gently places a hand on my cheek, giving me a soft smile. I smile back, and then we take our respective seats back at the table. Henry is beaming and also looks like he's holding back tears of his own.

"I told you so," he says so only I can hear.

All I can do is smile. I look over at Nath, and the look on his face I can only describe as pure joy for me – his favourite cousin and best friend. I wink at him, and he chuckles softly.

After everyone has filled their cups, Walter raises his for a toast.

"Well, cheers everybody. It's not quite Christmas, but this year feels like it's going to be the best one yet. Now, don't eat too much tonight because Lori has a feast ready for you tomorrow. To family, and to a no stress Chrissy!"

We laugh, and a chorus of cheers echoes as we clink our glasses together. I take a sip and audibly groan as the flavours of the wine hit my tongue.

"Oh my god, Lori. What is in this? It's the most delicious thing I've ever had in my entire life."

"It's a secret recipe. I'll share it with you one day." She winks.

Dinner is a platter of meats and cheeses, fruits and pastries, all laid out along the table for us to graze on. We dig in, falling into conversation about our favourite Christmas memories. When it's my turn to share, I pause for a moment to reflect and think back on Christmases past.

"I don't actually know if I'm remembering it, or I just think I do because I've seen home movies and photos, but I think my favourite Christmas was when I was about six years old. We set our video camera up and recorded ourselves putting up the Christmas tree. I just remember laughing so hard, Mum and Dad danced around the tree and they were so in love." I frown slightly; it's been a while since I've remembered what my parents were like when they were happy together.

"Christmas Day was so hot, and our air conditioner had broken, so we decided to spend Christmas down at the beach. We packed up all of our food and drinks into an esky, set up a picnic blanket under the marquee and spent the day in the sun and the sand. We played beach cricket with other families, swam until we were pruney, got a little bit sunburnt… By the time we were bundled into the car to head home, Gabi was asleep and I wasn't far off. It was the most relaxed, carefree Christmas Day."

"I remember that year. Mum came screaming down the beach for us to get out of the water because she saw a fin in the distance, thinking it was a shark," Nath chimes in.

"Oh yeah, and didn't it just end up being a pod of dolphins?" I ask, thinking back on the day.

"Sure was. She was so mad at us for not listening." He chuckles.

"Sounds like a true Aussie Christmas," says Walter. "Six years old though, surely you've had a few good ones since then?"

"A few, but honestly once my parents divorced it stopped being enjoyable and started to become stressful. No matter who I spent Christmas with, I was always going to be leaving someone alone on the day."

"That's a lot of guilt for a child to bare," says Lori.

"It was. I know it was never intentional, and I don't blame my parents for my grinch-ness, but it's hard to enjoy something when there's so much stress surrounding it. Add onto getting dumped on Christmas Eve a few years ago… it hasn't been great." I laugh.

Nath winces. "Hoo boy, that was not a fun Christmas."

"'Twas not the season to be jolly, let me tell you," I say dramatically.

"Well, I really hope that this Christmas is one that you will remember forever, in the best way. One that you will be able to use as an answer when someone else in the future asks you for your favourite Christmas story." Lori's eyes twinkle as she holds up her glass to me, and I smile back.

"Trust me, it's already one of the best Christmases I've ever had," I tell her.

"Wonderful."

***

The night goes on, and eventually it's time to FaceTime my family back home. It's technically Christmas morning for them, around 11am, so the family should be all together at Kathy's house by now. We set ourselves up in front of the Christmas tree, sitting by the fire and propping up my phone against a vase on the coffee table. Henry, Nath and I sit behind the camera, and Walter and Lori get comfy on the couch beside us.

"Ready?" Nath asks.

"Let's do it," I say, determined.

I pull up Mum's phone number and hit the video call icon. It rings for about three beats before she picks up, and when she does, her face is taking up half the screen and she's frowning in frustration at the camera.

"It's not working, I can't hear anything. Kathy, why can't I hear anything?"

"I don't know, Fiona, I'm no good with technology," Kathy yells from beside her.

"You can't hear anything because I haven't spoken yet," I say loudly.

Mum pulls her face back from the camera to see us better. "Oh, of course. Silly me. Hello, Claudia darling. Merry Christmas!" she sings.

"Merry Christmas, Mum. Merry Christmas, everyone!" I yell as she pans the camera across the whole kitchen. Everyone is there, except Gabi and Eric who are arriving a little later, choosing to spend Christmas morning as a family of three.

"Where's my boy?" Kathy asks, squeezing her face into the frame.

"I'm here, Mum. Merry Christmas." Nath waves into the camera.

"Merry Christmas! Or… Christmas Eve for you, isn't it? I still can't believe you left us for Christmas this year, Nath." Kathy pouts dramatically at the camera.

"Sorry. Adventure called my name. I couldn't let Claudia have all the fun." I punch him in the arm and he whines at me.

"You two are still children," Mum tuts.

I grin. "And we'll never change."

"How's your Christmas Eve going?" she asks.

"Really great, we've had a small dinner, some mulled wine. Now we're just relaxing in the lounge room by the fireplace. It's very calm," I not so subtly hint.

"That's lovely, Claudia. Is that…" She leans in closer to the camera to get a better look. "Is that a reindeer on your top that I can see? Claudia, are you wearing Christmas pyjamas?" she gasps, visibly in shock at my choice to dress festively.

"Claudia in Christmas clothes? Where? Let me see." Kathy shoves into view, and then Amanda, then the twins. Soon my screen is filled with family members scrambling to get a look at me in my Christmas outfit.

"Okay calm down, it's not that big a deal." I roll my eyes.

"You haven't worn anything Christmas-themed since you were a child," Mum says.

"Yes, well, times change," I tell her. What I really want to say is that this is the first Christmas I feel safe and comfortable enough to let my walls down to enjoy the day and be silly and wear Christmas apparel. I don't say that, of course.

"We're having fun, and that's all that matters," Henry pipes up.

"Oh! Hello, Henry," says Mum and Kathy.

"Henry!!!" the twins squeal.

"Hi everyone. Merry Christmas."

A chorus of "Merry Christmas" sounds from my phone as everyone takes it in turn to greet my boyfriend.

"And how's our little Grinch doing? You looking after her Henry?" butts in Uncle Ray.

"She's doing just fine. Amazing, in fact. Can we lay off the Grinch comments please, it's a little uncalled for."

"Ah pish-posh." Ray brushes off the request with a wave.

I clear my throat, directing the attention back to me.

"It's so beautiful here, Mum. The Christmas joy is infectious, and everyone here is so kind and welcoming."

"That's great to hear, darling. I had a feeling you would enjoy it there."

"Also say hi to Lori and Walter." I take the phone and turn the camera towards Henry's parents, who are cuddled up together on the couch, Lori nestled under Walter's arm. They're the picture-perfect couple, and it's so refreshing to see. They all greet each other, and then I turn the camera back to Henry, Nath and me.

"We won't keep you guys long, it's getting pretty late for us and I want to get a good night's sleep before tomorrow," I tell the family.

"Need your beauty sleep, Claudia? You look like you need it!" Ray cackles to himself. This time, I don't hold back my eye roll.

"Ray, come on man," Henry says defensively.

"Ah it's a joke. You young people can't take jokes anymore."

"It's not a joke if no one else laughs," Lori yells, and I bark out a laugh.

"Exactly, Uncle Ray. It's not a joke if it's at the expense of my self-esteem. But anyway, Merry Christmas, family! I hope you have a wonderful day. Stay cool, eat my share of the prawns, enjoy the afternoon swim. I'll see you in a few weeks when we get back."

"Merry Christmas, everyone." Nath waves at the camera.

"Merry Christmas!" The rest of our family pass the phone around so each person can say goodbye, and once it gets back to Mum, Henry and Nath give me a moment to say goodbye to her.

"Bye Mum, I hope you have a good day today. And I'm sorry I'm not there," I tell her.

"You don't have to say sorry, darling. It's just a day. Of course, I do miss you, but we will make up for it another time."

I know she means well, but it's exactly those types of statements that make me feel bad. Oddly enough, the guilt doesn't seem to hit as hard this time though. Perhaps being on another continent has helped, or maybe I'm starting to care just a little less.

"I know, I miss you too. Keep the rest of them in check today, seeing as Nath and I aren't there," I say, plastering on a smile that I hope doesn't appear forced.

"I will. Love you, my Claudia. Merry Christmas."

"Merry Christmas, Mum. Love you too."

We wave into the camera and I hang up, feeling a little bit lighter and not as guilty as I thought I'd feel.

"Well, that went pretty well," Henry says, rubbing a hand up and down my back.

"It did. Ray was only slightly annoying; Kathy didn't comment on my weight or ask when we're getting married… I take that as a win."

"A huge win."

"I'm sorry… they talk about your weight?" Lori exclaims.

"Every year. I'm too skinny, I'm too pudgy, I shouldn't eat so much… etcetera."

"That is so inappropriate," she says, shaking her head.

"Yeah, and that's just the tame comments. Sometimes it gets really bad," I tell her.

"It sure does. I love my parents but damn, they suck sometimes," Nath chimes in. "My dad is an old school kinda guy. No matter how many times I tell him something is inappropriate, he will claim I've gone soft and continue to make terrible comments." I know he has his own issues with his parents, and they're not my stories to share.

"Well, I can guarantee that for at least this Christmas no one will comment on anyone's weight, marital or parental status or food consumption. I promise you that." Lori stands, wiping her hands on the front of her jumper. "In this household, we love you for who you are, and we celebrate all of your wins, not just the ones society expects of you."

"That's right, like Claudia wearing matching Christmas pyjamas. That's a win," Nath says.

"Thanks, everyone. I hope you know that I do actually love my family, they're just a lot sometimes, and it's exhausting."

"We know," Henry says reassuringly.

"Okay, time to call Dad and then Gabi, and then that's everyone for the night."

We chat with my dad for a short while. He was busy preparing his pork roast, but it was good to hear his voice, and I swear I could smell the roasting meat through the phone. He makes a mean pork roast, especially at Christmas.

Gabi and Eric were too busy trying to wrangle Cooper to talk long, but we wished each other a happy Christmas, and promised to call again in a few days when things calm down.

"Well, that's that. Family obligations done, now I can just sit back and relax and maybe… enjoy myself," I jest.

Henry gives me a small smile. "It seems, Claudia, that you may be coming around to Christmas after all."

"Perhaps, we'll have to see what tomorrow brings."

TWENTY
Christmas Morning
2025

I wake to the sound of raucous laughter coming from downstairs, and Henry's arms wrapped around me, holding me tight. He stirs, pulling me in closer, the stubble on his chin gently scraping across my back. He gently kisses me on the shoulder, and I sigh into his body. So calm, content and happy.

"Merry Christmas, my sweet," he whispers against my skin.

"Hmm. Merry Christmas," I say back, refusing to open my eyes and start the day.

"Claudia…"

"Yeah?"

"It's snowing."

I sit upright in bed and immediately look out of the window to see snow falling softly, coating the ground and sticking.

"Oh my god, I'm getting a White Christmas," I say with glee.

"Yeah you are," he chuckles. "May it be a sign of a great day to come."

We all gave ourselves a bit of a sleep in, given how late we stayed up last night. The main perk of not having kids at Christmas time is that we can stay in bed for as long as we want, no 5am wake ups occurred in this household.

"This really is a bucket list moment. I never thought I'd get to do this."

Sliding up behind me, Henry pulls me against his chest so my back rests against his front. His body is still warm from sleep, and I snuggle into him.

"Now it's your reality, for whenever you want it," he says, nuzzling into my neck.

Snow on Christmas day, cutting our own tree, mulled wine by the fireplace… yeah, I can see myself wanting this. I let out a deep breath and relax into Henry's arms.

"So, question. How do you guys do the whole present thing? Do you all sit around in a circle and open them one by one? Or do you open them at the same time?"

"When I was little we opened them one at a time, only because it was just us three. But now, we normally don't open presents until after lunch. For us, the food is the main event. Plus it's more fun to open presents after a few wines."

"That sounds great. We all had to sit and wait for each of us to open presents one by one. And when we did it with the whole family, it took so damn long. Hence why I chose to spend Christmas mornings alone instead."

"Well, you're not alone anymore," he says, kissing my cheek.

Tilting my head back, I look into the depths of Henry's eyes and think about how we got here. About the first time we locked eyes at that party, how he jumped into the pool so that I wouldn't be alone, and how he hasn't left me alone since. This beautiful, selfless man who loves me in a way I never thought I could be loved. Who I now want to move across the world with. My heart aches for how much I love him.

"With you, I don't think I'll feel alone ever again."

Henry smiles and the butterflies in my stomach turn into a storm. I reach behind his neck and pull his mouth to mine, kissing him softly. His grip on my waist tightens as I deepen the kiss, brushing my tongue across his. He spins me around in his lap so I'm straddling him, and I slide my fingers into his hair, pulling gently.

"Claudia," he warns.

"Mmm?"

"You know what that does to me."

I smile devilishly. "I know."

He cups my face with both hands and ravages me with his mouth, kissing me desperately. I grind myself in his lap, causing him to inhale sharply, and I feel the hardness of him beneath me.

"As much as I want to bury myself inside of you right now…" he says against my lips, and a whimper escapes me at the thought. "We need to be downstairs soon. I promised Mum I would help with the food, and it's almost 10am."

"That means you have about ten minutes."

I grind myself once again, and his restraint snaps. In an instant, I'm flipped onto my back and he's hovering over me with a devilish gleam in his eye.

"I can do a lot in ten minutes," he says.

"Promise?"

He chuckles before finding the waistband of my pants and pulling them down fast, taking my underwear with them. I'm bare from the waist down, but that's not enough, because he makes quick work of my singlet top and throws it onto the floor. His pants soon follow. He's naked, I'm naked, and desperately wanting. He leans back on his knees to look at me, and I spread my legs open so he can take all of me in.

"Merry Christmas, Henry."

He locks eyes with me, slowly, gliding his hand up and down his erection and causing me to squirm under his gaze.

"You are so fucking pretty," he growls.

"And I'm all yours."

He dives right in, his mouth on me in an instant, wasting no time getting to the point. And the point is to make me come as quickly as possible, it seems, because I'm writhing beneath him within seconds. I'm so turned on by this man all the damn time, so there is no resistance when he slides two fingers into me, causing my hips to buck.

"Best. Christmas. Ever," I pant, getting closer to climax.

"Just wait until I stuff your stocking, sweetheart."

A laugh bursts out of me but is soon replaced by a moan as he coaxes my orgasm to the surface, sending me crashing down as his fingers work me and his mouth devours me. Before I can even fully recover, he flips me onto my stomach and brings my arse up into the air. With a soft caress of his fingers, he spreads me open and buries himself to the hilt.

"Fuck, Claudia, you're so wet for me. Better grab that pillow – I don't want anyone else to hear your screams."

I do as he says and pull the pillow to me, covering my mouth when he starts to move. In and out, ever so slowly, he builds up the pace and I'm whimpering. Soon, he's pounding into me so hard he needs to hold onto the bedframe so it doesn't hit the bedroom wall. I have to bite into the pillow to stop my screams from echoing throughout the house, because the pleasure he's wringing from me has me seeing stars. He's hitting every pleasurable spot inside me, and when he reaches around and gently caresses my clit, he sends me spiralling over the edge again. His hand grips my hip so tight and his speed increases to a punishing level, before he reaches his own end and spills himself inside of me.

Leaning down over the top of me, he trails kisses along my spine as we each try to catch our breaths. He gently pulls out of me, careful not to make too much of a mess, and walks into our ensuite bathroom to grab a cloth, while I collapse onto my belly on the bed, perfectly satiated.

Henry comes back with a warm wash cloth and cleans me up, before tending to his own needs. The act of a true gentleman.

"Well…" I say as I lie there, slowly coming down from my orgasm. "We did that in seven minutes. Now you can still go help your mum."

Henry laughs and gives my arse a light smack. "I think I want to start Christmas like that every morning from now on." He lies down next to me and tenderly brushes my hair out of my face.

"We're in agreement."

He leans in and gives me a quick kiss, before getting up and putting his pyjamas back on. I sit up, feeling a delicious ache in my body from the quickie.

"Oh and also… stuff my stocking?"

Henry throws his head back and laughs, and I can't help but do the same. "Sorry, it came to me in the moment and I had to say it."

"It was brilliant. I just didn't know that I could laugh and come at the same time."

He smirks. "Now you know."

"I'm going to take a shower and get ready for the day. Tell your parents I'll be down soon."

"I will. Enjoy your shower."

He kisses me on the top of my head and heads downstairs. I hear his parents greet him and wish him a Merry Christmas , and I smile to myself. Turning on the shower, I stand in the mirror and look at my reflection. Slightly dishevelled, flushed and smiling from ear to ear. A completely different person to the one I was two years ago. What a contrast it is to wake up with someone I love on Christmas morning and not feel anxious or stressed about how the day is going to go, or what someone is going to say. I step into the shower and let the hot water rush over me, washing away the guilt I've carried for years and allowing myself to enjoy the day exactly how it's meant to be.

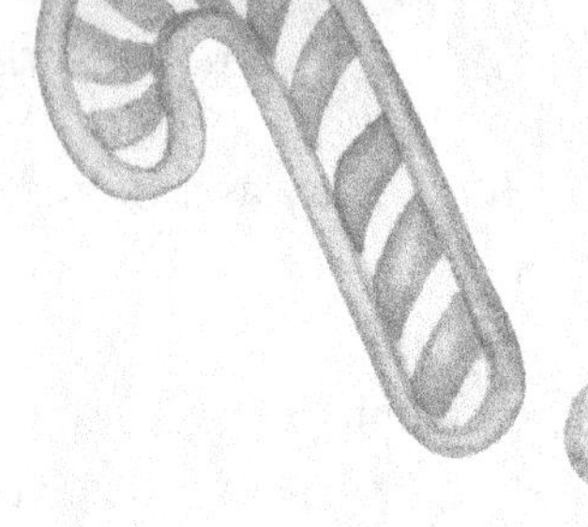

TWENTY-ONE
Christmas Day
2025

The stairs creak beneath my feet as I descend into the living room. I'm feeling fresh and ready for the day after an orgasm and a hot shower. My senses are immediately overloaded as soon as I reach the landing, with an abundance of Christmas food being cooked and prepared by Lori and Henry. Nath is sitting at the dining table, munching on a gingerbread cookie, when he sees me poking my head into the room.

"Wow, Claudia."

All heads turn in my direction, pinning me to the spot. They all smile brightly at me, Henry leaning against the kitchen cupboard and giving me a wink.

"What?" I ask.

"You look beautiful," Lori says, coming over to give me a hug. "Merry Christmas, darling girl."

"Merry Christmas, Lori. And you too, Walter." I reach over and hug the man, who already appears to have helped himself to some of the Christmas ham.

"What Lori said. A true Christmas beauty." He gives me a kiss on the cheek, and a blush spreads across my face.

"Thank you."

"Two days of Christmas-themed outfits in a row, Claud. It's a bloody miracle," Nath says.

"Let's just not make a big deal out of it, okay? For the first time in forever, I don't feel like I want to vomit on Christmas morning, let's keep it that way."

He holds his hands up in surrender. "Okay. I can shut up. You look cute, cousin. Nice to see you dress up for once."

I roll my eyes but walk over to him for a hug.

"Truly, Claud, it suits you. This place and Christmas," he whispers so only I can hear.

"Thank you. I'm so glad you're here with me," I whisper back.

I didn't think my outfit was over the top for Christmas, but I guess a bold red lip does stand out when it's not something I usually wear. I went with a simple, oversized white knitted jumper, sprinkled with small gold snowflakes, paired with black tights. I finished the look with the red lipstick and tied half of my curls up in a big red bow. I felt cozy and cute, perfect for my first happy Christmas in years.

Henry walks over to me and places an arm around my waist. "You do look beautiful."

"Even more beautiful than earlier this morning?" I tease.

"Your beauty is a spectrum, one I am truly blessed to see in its entirety."

"Well…" I clear my throat. "Aren't you full of compliments today."

"Always."

As I lean in for a kiss, I hear the distinctive click of a camera and look over to see Lori taking a photo of us on her phone, looking giddy.

"You two are just so cute together!" she squeaks.

"Mum, I'm still in my pyjamas," Henry whines.

"Well then go and get dressed! I plan on taking many photos today. Wear something handsome."

"Okay, okay. Jeez. I'll be back soon."

Henry races upstairs and within minutes I can hear water running from the pipes. It's only now that I'm down here that I realise how *not* sound proof this house is. Mortified and turning even redder, I busy myself by making a coffee and sitting next to Nath at the table.

"Why are you blushing?" he asks.

"I'm not."

"Is it because now you realise the whole house probably heard you getting railed this morning?"

Coffee hits the back of my throat and I choke, almost spraying it all over Nath's clean blue jumper.

"Oh my god. Please tell me they didn't…"

"Don't worry, I started playing some Christmas carols before you reached your crescendo. They didn't hear anything."

"I can never show my face here again."

"Nah, you're fine. Those two were busy dancing and singing to each other to notice. I, however, am scarred for life. But also… get it, girl. Proud of you."

"Please stop talking."

Nath laughs, and we both take a sip of coffee and relax into our chairs.

"This is so different to home, isn't it?" he says.

"So different. My mind and body don't know what to do."

"I say, when it's acceptable, we pour ourselves a wine and enjoy the day without overthinking it."

"Great idea."

"Claudia, would you be able to help me with brussels sprouts please?" Lori asks.

"Of course."

Henry doesn't take long in the shower and comes back downstairs looking very handsome in a dark green knit jumper and tan pants. I continue to try and help in the kitchen, but I soon find that I'm more of a hinderance than a help and sit back down with Nath. After a while, we decide to transition from coffee to beer, because it's Christmas and there are no rules about when it's appropriate to start drinking.

***

"Eat up, everyone!"

The sound of cutlery clinking against plates, the pouring of wine, and the happy laughter of everyone at the table fills the room. Everything looks absolutely perfect, and Lori has put on an absolute feast for us all. In the middle of the table is a huge roast turkey, big enough to feed a family of twelve, let alone our group of five. There's fluffy mashed potato and brussels sprouts, honey-roasted carrots, baked ham and a whole lot of gravy. My mouth waters, and I don't know where to start.

"Lori, this is incredible. You have outdone yourself," I tell her as I heap a spoonful of mashed potato onto my plate.

"It's my pleasure. Cooking for family is my favourite thing in the world to do."

"We've got enough food here to last us a week, if not more," Nath says.

"You'd be surprised. Between these two," she points between Henry and Walter, "this is usually cleared up within about three days. I'm guessing two days now, with our two additional guests."

"By the time we're finished, I won't want to see another turkey again until next Thanksgiving," Henry says.

"Oh Thanksgiving. That's a holiday I'm going to have to wrap my head around if I'm going to move here."

Silence spreads across the table, and I realise my error as Henry attempts to smother his smile.

"Uh…"

"Did you just say move? Here?" Lori asks.

I look at Henry, and he just shrugs. "You might as well tell them."

Lori and Walter are looking between us, confusion written on their faces.

"Well… after being here and seeing the town, and spending time with you all, I've decided that once Henry has finished his time in Australia, I'm going move back here with him."

There's a pause, and then a scream of joy erupts from Lori's mouth. I swear I hear a car alarm go off two streets over.

"Oh my god! Really? You're moving here?" She turns to Henry. "You're coming home?"

"I am. We are. Eventually. I still have a lot I want to see and do in Australia, but when I'm ready, we'll move back home. You can both retire, and I'll take over the bakery."

"This is so wonderful to hear," Walter says with a grin.

"I have to admit, when you told us you'd met an Australian girl I was nervous you'd want to move there permanently."

"And I would have, if she'd asked me to," Henry says, reaching for my hand and giving it a squeeze.

"But instead, I fell in love with Almonte. We still need to look into the logistics of it all, but that's the plan."

"Oh darling girl, you have made this old woman very, very happy," Lori says, tears rimming her eyes.

"I wouldn't have even thought it possible, if it weren't for how kind and supportive you both are. So thank you, for making me feel like this could be a home for me."

"Always, darling. We will always have a spot for you here," she says.

"Okay, enough with the sap, let's dig in before our lunch gets cold," Nath interrupts, a smile on his face. He's so happy for me, and though I will miss him like crazy when I do eventually move, I'm so thankful for his support.

"Cheers, everyone, and Merry Christmas."

Falling quiet, we dig into our food, the only sounds are the scraping of cutlery and the groans of delight when taking a bite.

"I could drink this gravy," I say, spooning a second serving of it onto my mashed potatoes.

"I did one year. Mum caught me sneaking around the kitchen on Christmas night, gravy boat tipped up into my mouth." Henry laughs.

"We can share one tonight." I wink.

"Claudia, dear, do you want some more? There's another pot on the stove. I always make extra because this one drowns everything in gravy, and it appears you two are a match, in more ways than one," Lori says, pointing directedly at my plate which is now swimming in the delicious brown sauce.

I swallow the mouthful of potato that started to feel stuck in my throat. I'm so used to being judged by what I eat or how much food is on my plate, I don't know how to react by someone offering me more, without judgement or criticism. It's so refreshing I could cry.

"I'm okay for now but thank you. We're just a couple of fiends when it comes to gravy."

"That we are," Henry adds.

Silence falls once again as we finish our meal, going back for seconds and thirds, until everyone is slumped in their seats, rubbing their bellies from the fullness.

"I am so glad I wore tights today," I moan. I'm so full, but so happy.

"Alright, gents. It's time," Henry says to Walter and Nath.

They look at each other and nod, and then, in perfect synchronisation, pop the top button of their pants and lower their zipper.

"Oh yeah, that's better," Walter breathes. They all slump further into their seats, Lori and I laughing at the sight before us.

"Can we go play in the snow now that we've eaten?" Nath asks. "This is my first White Christmas too, and I want to make the most of it by kicking your arse in a snowball fight."

"Okay. It's on. Let's go." I stand from the table, ready to fight.

"Five more minutes," Henry says, pointing to his stomach. "I need to digest a little bit longer."

"Wine helps," Lori says as she pours him another glass.

I hold mine up to her as well for a refill, and she winks at me as she does.

"So, are we playing in teams or is it every man for himself?" I ask.

"Every man for himself, obviously," Henry scoffs. "I must reign supreme."

Fifteen minutes later, we're standing in the backyard, covered head to toe in coats, beanies and gloves. I blow into my hands to warm them, because despite the beauty of snow on Christmas day, it's fucking freezing.

"The rules are, there are no rules. You attack until someone surrenders. Last man standing is the winner. Got it?" Henry says.

We all nod in agreement.

"Okay. Mum, would you like to do the honours?"

"Alright everyone, into your positions. Fight starts in five…" We all run in different directions, vying for the best vantage point for attack and defence. "Four… three… two… one. Attack!"

Snowballs begin flying in every direction, hitting trees and walls, all in varying sizes. I'm clearly an amateur, because my snowballs barely hold together before they break apart on impact. I manage to hit Nath on the shoulder, before I'm bombarded with about six snowballs from every corner of the yard. I refuse to yield, so I duck for cover behind a tree and reassess my strategy. After a minute, Lori yields due to snow going down the back of her coat and into her shirt. Walter then pulls out because his stomach starts cramping from eating too much. Soon, it's down to Nath, Henry and me.

I hear a "psst" from Henry's direction and look over the edge of my hiding spot to see him gesture towards Nath, before pointing between the two of us, and then running a thumb across his neck. Destroy Nath, got it. I give him a thumbs up and form a few snowballs to top up my ammunition. I look over at Henry again, and I think he's gesturing for me to distract and he'll attack, so I nod and get ready to make a run for it. I count down with my fingers, and when I get to one I sprint out from behind my tree. Nath takes the bait and launches a volley of snowballs in my direction, but the plan works because Henry sneaks up behind him and piles armfuls of snow onto him, until finally Nath yields.

"No fair. You guys said this wasn't a team game," he sulks as he walks back over to the house.

"You're right, we did say that," Henry says, and I turn in time to see him run towards me, before tackling me into a pile of fresh snow. We hit the ground with a dull thud, and I wriggle to try and get out of his grip. Then, the arsehole starts to tickle me.

"Oh my god, Henry! No! Tickling!" I scream, but he doesn't give up. I'm scream laughing at this point, and he slowly makes his way down to tickle me behind the knees, and I have no option but to surrender.

"Okay! Okay! You win. I yield. Please stop." I laugh.

He stops immediately and raises his arms in the air like he's won Olympic gold.

"I am once again the champion! I shall always remain unde feated!" he roars.

I chuck a handful of snow in his face and he starts spluttering.

"Oops, it slipped." I grin devilishly.

Wiping the snow clinging to his lashes, he smirks at me and leans down for a kiss. We're surrounded by a blanket of white. I'm freezing cold but choosing to ignore the bite of it, because I feel like in this moment, I could be the main character of a Christmas movie, and looking into his baby blue eyes, I feel like I'm home.

"Let's get you back inside and warmed up," he says gently. I can't do anything but nod. He stands, reaching his arm out to pull me up with him. We walk back inside and I immediately sigh with relief, the warmth of the fireplace defrosting my bones. Lori has concocted another batch of mulled wine, which is simmering gently on the stove.

"Once everyone has warmed up, pour yourself some wine and then head back into the living room. It's present time," she sings.

I shed my coat and my gloves and stand close to the fireplace, holding my hands out to defrost my frozen fingers. Once I start to get feeling back into my limbs, I pour myself a cup of wine and find a spot in the living room, on the couch next to Henry. I take a sip of wine and let the warm and festive flavours take over my senses.

"Okay, now that we're all warm and boozed up, let's get started. Before we open our gifts, traditionally, we each go around and say something we are grateful for. Who would like to start?"

"I will," Walter says. "I'm grateful for each and every one of you, and I'm grateful to be hearing so many Australian accents at Christmas time. It has been a long time, and it's bringing up memories of home. So, thank you."

"No worries," Nath and I both say at the same time, and everyone laughs.

"I'm grateful to you, Lori and Walter, for opening up your home and allowing me to be here for Christmas, and for giving my cousin the Christmas day she deserves," Nath says, raising his cup. I smile at him and blow a kiss in his direction.

"Lori?"

"Well…" She clears her throat. "I'm grateful to you, Claudia, for loving my son. I have never seen him so happy, the way he looks at you reminds me of my own young love with Walter. It's the look of a love that will last a lifetime. Thank you for loving him the way you do."

The amount of times this woman has made me tear up since being here…

"Oh Lori." I smile. "You're going to make me cry again. You raised an incredible man, and I'm so lucky to be able to call him mine."

They all look at me, and I pause for a moment to think. There is so much I'm grateful for, it's hard to narrow it down.

"I'm grateful for all of you. Thank you, from the bottom of my heart, for embracing me as your family, and for giving me the best Christmas I've had since I was a small child. I can never thank you enough. Also, for giving me the greatest gift, and that is your son. I think I have truly met my match, and it's all thanks to you, Lori and Walter." A tear slips down Lori's cheek, and I get up to give her a hug. She squeezes me tight, before I lean over to give Walter a hug too. He holds me longer than he ever has, and even his eyes appear to be lined with tears, not that he would ever admit it.

Henry looks at me with so much love and adoration, I feel like I'm burning under his gaze.

"My turn," he whispers.

I sit back down next to him, and he takes my hand in his.

"I'm grateful, for this amazing woman right next to me." He turns and angles his body so he's facing me, still holding delicately onto my hand. "Claudia, you are the most down to earth, intelligent, beautiful and charming woman I have ever met in my life. Every morning that I wake up next to you, I consider the greatest day of my life."

"Henry…" I whisper. His words making me tear up once more.

"Do you remember our first date?" he asks, and I nod, too scared to say anything in case I start to cry even more.

"On that date, you told me you didn't want anyone to waste your time. You told me exactly what you wanted in life. And sweetheart, I want to give you everything you've ever wanted, if you'll let me…"

Henry rises from the couch and steps in front of me, his eyes never leaving mine, before slowly dropping to one knee.

A chorus of gasps ripples throughout the room, but all I can hear is the pounding of my own heartbeat. With tears in his eyes, Henry reaches into his back pocket and pulls out a small velvet box. He opens the lid, revealing the most beautiful ring I could have imagined nestled within.

"Claudia. You are my brightest light, my best friend, and my truest love. Will you, on this magical Christmas day, make me the happiest man in the world. Will you marry me?"

My face falls into my hands as sobs overtake me, my shoulders trembling with the weight of my emotion. I nod through the tears, and then throw myself into his lap, wrapping my arms tightly around his neck.

"Is that a yes?" he asks, laughing nervously.

"Yes, yes, yes," I cry.

He pulls the ring from the box and I hold out my trembling left hand. It slides on seamlessly, an absolutely perfect fit, and I stare at it in disbelief. A thin gold band holding three stones: a marquise-cut diamond in the middle, bordered by two pale green gemstones.

Lori is audibly sobbing from the other couch, with Walter rubbing her back in an effort to console her. He appears to have given up trying to hide his emotions, because he too has tears streaming down his face. And Nath, my beautiful cousin and best friend, has his phone in hand capturing the moment, also shedding a tear.

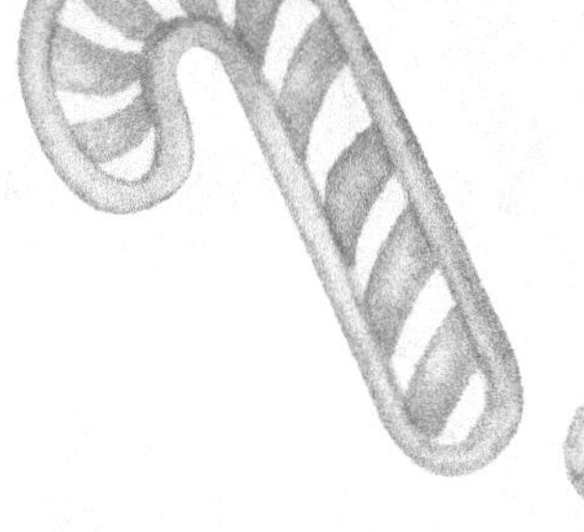

TWENTY-TWO
A Happy Ending

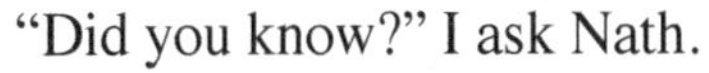

"Did you know?" I ask Nath.

"I did." He smirks. "He may have mentioned something to me yesterday."

I look to Henry, who is still smiling from ear to ear. "Cheeky," I say.

"I thought you might want to remember this moment."

"How could I ever forget?"

"Oh Claudia!" Lori wails, leaping off the couch and embracing me. "You're officially part of the family now. I'm so, so happy."

"It's an honour to be a part of your family, Lori." I hold her to me, hugging her tighter than I ever have before.

Walter stands up and scoops us both up. "You chose a good one, Henry. Good job on not screwing it up and locking her down."

"Thanks… I think," Henry laughs.

In a rush, Lori runs into the kitchen and brings back a bottle of champagne. "I've been saving this bottle for a special occasion. Let's open it."

"Sounds good to me," I say. "It's too early to call my family to tell them, and I'll probably need a glass or five before I do anyway."

We each receive a glass as Walter pops the cork.

"We only get these champagne flutes out for very special occasions," he says with a wink, pouring each of us a decent serving of bubbly.

"Well, cheers to you both. Congratulations, and may every Christmas forward be as magical and full of love as this one," Lori says.

"I think it will be hard to beat," I tell her. "Dare I say it… but I think this has been the best Christmas I have ever had."

"Does that mean… I achieved my mission?" Henry gasps, clutching at his chest dramatically.

"Normally I would hate to admit this, but yes."

Henry fist pumps the air, looking like an absolute dork.

"What was the mission?" Walter asks.

"To make her fall in love with Christmas again, an impossible feat," Nath chuckles.

"And yet… I succeeded," Henry boasts.

"Hard not to fall in love with Christmas when you get proposed to." Nath smirks.

"Actually, even without the proposal, he would have achieved his mission," I say.

They all look at me, waiting for me to continue.

"You've all helped, but this truly has been the best Christmas. There has been no pressure, or guilt, or stress. I've had fun, and for the first time in years I can hand on my heart say that I've truly enjoyed not just the day itself, but the lead up to it as well." I pause to gather my thoughts.

"Christmas just hits different here, and I am sad that the best Christmas I've had in years has been away from my family, and maybe the guilt of that will hit later, but I finally feel like I'm allowed to be excited about it again. I'm allowed to love it again.

And after today, I do. I love Christmas. This place has healed my inner child, and I wish little Claudia could see me now, so I could tell her that it does get better."

No one says anything, but Henry takes my hand and kisses my knuckles. Everyone lifts their glasses in the air, my engagement ring sparkling on my finger as if trying to outshine the lights on the Christmas tree.

"To Henry and Claudia. And to loving Christmas again."

"To us," Henry says, voice low. "To forever."

I don't think I can speak again without crying, so I just clink my glass against his, and Nath's, and my soon to be mother and father-in-law.

I take a sip, the champagne bubbles dancing against my lips and bursting across my tongue, and sigh in contentment.

After we finish the bottle and the Christmas presents are unwrapped, Henry and I excuse ourselves and make our way upstairs for a private moment before calling my family.

The room is quiet, and we say nothing as we climb on top of the bed. I curl into his side and our legs tangle together. Lying there together, neither of us feel the need to fill the silence. His thumb traces circles on the back of my hand, and my heart rate slowly starts to return to its steady rhythm.

"You were shaking," I murmur, smiling into his chest.

He laughs softly. "I was terrified. Not of asking you, I was fairly certain you would say yes. Just... of the moment. Of wanting it too much."

"And now?" I ask, looking up at him.

"Now I'm just happy. I don't think I have ever felt this level of happiness." His eyes soften.

The proposal itself wasn't a grand gesture. There were no fireworks, no giant surprise party, no runway of petals and a giant *'Will you marry me?'* sign.

"It was everything I could have wanted, and more."

We lie there, wrapped in each other's arms for a heartbeat longer, before Henry shifts beneath me, pulling out his phone.

"Ready?" he asks.

"As I'll ever be. Can we call everyone and get it all out of the way? I want to ravish my fiancé," I say, grinning.

He chuckles. "Let's get started then."

First, we call my mum. I hold my hand up to the camera, so the ring is the first thing she sees. She answers swiftly…

"Merry Christmas again, you two! Oh hang on, why can't I see anything…" She sees my hand and glares at the screen, as if not quite registering what she's seeing.

"Are you two… wait. What is that? Claudia…"

I hold up my hand next to my face so all she can see is my ring and my grin.

There's a beat of stunned silence.

Then a squeal loud enough to rattle the ornaments.

"Oh my god! He proposed? Oh Claudia, I'm so happy for you!" She's laughing and crying at the same time, covering her mouth with her hand. "I need to sit down."

The rest of the call blurs into rapid-fire questions, as she demands every single detail about the proposal. I send her the video that Nath took, and she watches it as she's on the phone with us, crying even more. We manage to end the call, with a promise to call again after we've had some sleep, and I make her promise not to say anything to anyone until after we call the rest of the family.

Next, I call my dad. He answers calmly, as always, but the moment I tell him, I hear the catch in his breath.

"I was hoping," he says, voice soft and shaking just a little. "I was really hoping. He's a good one. Henry, you take good care of my daughter. I'm so happy for you both."

We make several more calls after that. Gabi, who cries so hard I can't decipher anything she says. Frankie, who screams so loud I have to put her on mute. As soon as we tell Aunty Kathy, she starts demanding details about the wedding date.

"Actually, Kathy, we're eloping. And we have to go to bed now, goodnight!" Henry says cheerfully, swiftly ending the call.

"Oh my god, I can't believe you just said that. She's going to be mortified." I laugh.

"Let her sweat for a bit." He shrugs. "We'll add something to the group chat after the calls to clarify."

Every phone call we make fills the room with more joy, more laughter, more love. Eventually, my yawns outweigh my smiles, and after ending the call with my Aunty Amanda and EJ, we just sit there. The screen has gone dark, and the silence is buzzing with energy.

"It's official," I say.

"Yep. Now everyone knows."

I glance down at my ring again, then lean onto his shoulder, letting out a breath and relaxing into the silence. Henry shoots a quick message into the family group chat, along with the proposal video, and reassures everyone that no we won't be eloping, it was a joke, and we will update them on wedding plans soon, and to let us just enjoy the engagement.

We have a quick shower together, embracing each other in the purest of forms and connecting in a way that soon has me weeping with joy. There will be no ravishing tonight – I'm too caught up in my emotions – so we crawl into bed and curl around each other, skin to skin, heart to heart.

"We could, you know, elope. If you wanted to," Henry whispers into the dark.

"Hmm. I haven't really considered it. But honestly, let's not even think about it yet. I want to enjoy this moment right here and now. People always seem to want to rush into the next stage of something. I want to bask in this joy before the stress of wedding planning takes over."

"Sounds perfect to me. I love you, sweetheart."

"I love you too."

As we turn out the light and settle into the quiet, Henry's hand finds mine beneath the covers. The room is still, and all I can hear is the steady rhythm of our breathing. I didn't know I could feel so happy and still want to cry. This Christmas has given me more than I ever knew to hope for.

I drift off to sleep with a smile on my face, certain that no matter how many Christmases come and go, whether they are good or bad, this will be the one that I carry with me, forever.

ACKNOWLEDGEMENTS

Never in my wildest dreams did I think I'd write a Christmas book, yet here we are.

Like Claudia, I've always found Christmas more stressful than joyful, and not quite the magical experience it's often made out to be. I wanted to write a Christmas story that felt realistic and relatable, especially for my fellow eldest daughters and anyone from a split family who knows how complicated this time of year can be.

I also set out to write about an Australian Christmas, something I feel is sorely underrepresented. While the story ended up taking my characters abroad, it was rooted in my own feelings: Australian Christmases aren't exactly romantic or whimsical. It's hot, the bugs are relentless, and the vibe often feels far from festive. So, I took Claudia somewhere else, somewhere where that could help shift her perspective.

What came out of it was a Christmas love story about healing your inner child and rediscovering the joy of Christmas. And now? I've made it my mission to experience a White Christmas of my own, to hopefully give me the magical Christmas experience I crave deep down.

I would like to firstly thank my readers who have stuck around and supported me since my debut. Your excitement for my second release gives me the confidence to keep writing.

I want to thank my partner Matt. I asked you to bully and

bribe me into completing my work and you did. Thank you for being the first to read this book and give a man's perspective (I've never thought so hard about a toilet flush before). Thank you for loving me and supporting me and cheering me on as always. I love you.

To my family. Thank you for making Christmas feel full, loud, and unforgettable in all the best ways. Sorry Nanna, this one is also a little bit naughty, you might want to skim read a few pages!

Thank you to my beta team: Jess, Matt, Carly, Caitlin, Vida and Victoria. Your feedback was invaluable and instrumental in writing this story. ILYSM.

Thank you to my girls, Jess, Briony, Etta and Britt. My life is richer with you in it and I'm so lucky to call you my friends.

Thank you to my amazing editor Gabby (@gcdeditorial). You are a queen. I can't wait to work with you again on future projects. You're an Adelaide girlie too, and we have to support local!

Thank you to Talia for my formatting, I was planning on doing it myself this time around and you saved me from so much stress. I appreciate you! And also a thank you to Ivanna for capturing my characters so perfectly. Your artwork is impeccable every single time.

Thank you to the indie romance community and bookstores who support me and cheer for me, especially when I'm feeling the self-doubt creep in. An especially big thank you if you stock my books in your store, you have no idea the impact you have.

I would also like to thank Taylor Swift for not only providing the background music to most of my writing sessions, but for also releasing "Eldest Daughter" right as I was going through my last edits. This song destroyed me and encapsulated this story in every possible way.

And finally, thank you, the reader, for giving me a chance as an author and picking up this book. By supporting my work you continue to support my dream and for that I will forever be grateful.

CLAUDIA'S CHOCOLATE CHIP COOKIES

This recipe is inspired by the Chunky Chocolate Cookies from the FamilyCircle Best of Kids Cooking cook book, which was a staple in my household since I was a child.
Enjoy!

Ingredients:
- ½ cup of brown sugar
- 1 egg
- 1/3 cup of neutral oil
- 2 tablespoons (or more, you do you boo) of hot chocolate powder or Nesquik
- ½ cup of self-raising flour
- ½ cup of plain flour
- ¾ cup of chopped up chocolate of choice (milk, dark or white… or all. Go for your life actually.)

Method:
1. Preheat oven to 180 degrees Celsius (fan forced) or 200 degrees Celsius (not fan forced).
2. Lightly grease two oven trays with butter or oil, or line with baking paper.
3. Place sugar, egg and oil into a bowl and mix well.
4. Sift into the bowl the flour and hot chocolate powder or Nesquik.
5. Add in chopped chocolate pieces and mix through gently.
6. In the bowl, knead lightly with your hands to form a soft dough.
7. Roll the dough into balls using one tablespoon of the mixture.

8. Place the balls on a try approximately 4cm apart (this will prevent them from sticking together).
9. Bake one tray at a time for 12 – 15 minutes. The cookies should rise gently and look fluffy, with some slight cracking on the outside. If after 15 minutes they still aren't cooked, go by gut instinct. (I'm not a chef; this is just what I do at home lol).
10. Once cooked, remove from the oven and leave the cooking sitting on the oven tray for five minutes before removing and placing them on a cooling rack.
11. Dig in, try not to eat them all at once!

ABOUT THE AUTHOR

Fuelled by her passion for storytelling, a strong cup of coffee and a good laugh, **Emily Nicole** is a new voice in the world of Australian romance. Her love for reading began at a young age, and as she reached adulthood, resulted in a dream career as a librarian. She is constantly surrounded by books. When she's not at work, reading, or writing, she's busy listening to Taylor Swift, reviewing books on her Bookstagram account and interacting with fellow book lovers.